Books of The Lost Tribe:

The Lost Tribe: The Traveller
The Lost Tribe: Sins of the Father
The Lost Tribe: Darkest Hour
The Lost Tribe: Revelations

This novel is dedicated to my love,
Alisha – Keep the light on.

I'd also like to thank all of those in
Mick's universe who kept up the faith.

Thank you all, once and again.

All inquiries, kudos, criticisms, or comments should be directed to plivey@yahoo.com

PETER IVEY's

THE LOST TRIBE:

SINS OF THE

FATHER

Before

Mick's world has been turned on its head once more. After gaining his powers and finding others like himself, Mick continued his quest for answers…who are the lost tribe? Where did they all come from? His search for meaning brought him in contact with a mysterious being called Apostos who seemed determined to keep the answers from him. Through Apostos, Mick was brought into contact with others like himself. Some joined him in his cause to find meaning and answers, yet others seemed hell-bent on standing in his way with their own agenda. Thus, Mick learned of the Kingdom, a group of his people led by a powerful woman named Lethia. While their plan seemed to be about nothing more than destruction and chaos, Mick soon learned that there was a purpose behind the path of devastation courtesy of a powerful oracle in the service of the Kingdom.

It was then that he realized that he and his companions had become pawns of Apostos and that Apostos cared little for what happened to Mick and his adopted family. After a terrible injury at the torturous hands of the Kingdom, Mick became driven by revelations about his past learned during his captivity to finally confront Apostos and get the answers that had remained hidden.

In the startling conclusion, Mick fought Apostos, bringing him low with the destructive nature of the truth that Mick had learned. In the aftermath, Mick was spirited away by the man behind the curtain, a powerful entity called Father, who claimed to be the creator of all the worlds and the architect of Mick and his lost tribe. He revealed that he had guided Mick on his path to become his champion against the Kingdom. He bequeathed to Mick the power to vanquish forever the darkness inside the Kingdom that gave them their power, with the promise that he would forge them all a world of their own in return for Mick's service. However, he also promised that failure on Mick's part would mean the doom of all the worlds if Father had to take on the task himself. Taking on the burden of what he had learned and the power he had been given, Mick was sent back to rally his friends to take on the Kingdom and save the worlds from destruction…

THE BEAST

The boy hung in the stocks, his wrists restrained, his feet barely scraping the dirt as he feebly tried to keep himself from strangling where his neck was shackled. Blood-streaked spittle hung from his ruined lips, but there were no tears in his eyes. He had stopped crying a very long time ago. The tent was dark, lit only by the flickering light of torches from outside the entrance off to his left. The flame reflected off of various metal objects in the room…several brass bowls filled with water were set out on one table and another held a variety of unpleasant-looking sharp instruments that were the tools of the trade in his father's business. His eyelids felt very heavy. Soon, he would either die in his sleep, or die eyes wide open.

"Wake up, you little monster," his father's voice said.

He felt his father's strong hand pull his head up in the stocks by the dark locks of his hair and the fresh pain helped to revive him. His father, freshly shaven, steely-eyed, portly and dressed in boiled leather and a red cloak stood in front of him, grinning at his discomfort. He cried out and made to bite at his hand. His father withdrew it and struck him across the chin. His lip exploded and more blood joined the glorious river that seeped from his mouth. Whether or not he realized it, his father had taught him to relish such moments. He grinned and a peel of laughter escaped his bloody lips.

"What is there to laugh at for you, boy? Your whore of a mother is in the ditch and you're moments away from being fed to the dogs! What are you laughing at?"

"A man with a very small cock," he replied, "Or so she always said."

The blow came square against his nose, detonating it like a ripe tomato across his face. *At least I won't be conscious enough to feel myself being ripped apart…*

"Don't you pass out on me yet, you foul little freak!" his father growled.

He whistled and one of his men dragged in one of the hounds from the kennel. The boy's eyes widened. His father took the hound and stroked it beneath the chin.

"From the look on your pretty face, I know that you recognize this beast?" his father asked.

The boy said nothing and glared at his tormentor.

"Well? Speak up! What do you call this mongrel?"

The boy said nothing.

"You will tell me his name if you love him, boy," he said, pulling a knife from beneath his cloak, "or I'll slit his goddamn throat."

"His name is Falkir!" the boy spat.

"You love him?"

He knew he was beaten. It was best just to play out the game. He would not give up his tears…he would not!!

"Yes!!"

"Then let me show you what I love," his father said.

He slit the hound's throat in one deft and terrible motion and the beast collapsed to the floor, its eyes rolling feebly, as if trying to reason out its death.

"Falkir!!" the boy cried.

His father laughed and kicked the dog's corpse.

"Falkir…" the man in the stocks mused.

The stocks disappeared. In the boy's place, I stood; the boy that was once me was gone, long dead and buried. This was no mere memory! What transpired here? Another of Apostos' tricks, perhaps? I pulled my favorite dagger from its sheath at my side and put it to the throat of my father's shade. He had been my first prey and it brought joy to my heart to see him under my knife again. He smiled a gaping grin and his face began to melt. I let go of him and watched his entire body dissolve and begin to reform. A trick, indeed!

"I know, I know," a voice said, "You were probably expecting horns, a tail, or a whiff of sulfur?"

I moved back, giving myself room to move and attack if need be…the figure was dressed very much like Jack, in a black suit, slick black hair and clean shaven. His eyes were black as well and the irises were huge. His gaze followed me as I paced around him. I flicked the dagger around, seeing if it pulled his gaze to it instead. It did not.

"You're in my head," I said, "Imitating a man that I despised when he was alive and whose memory I defecate upon since I sent him to molder in the earth. Who are you and what do you want?"

The man walked over and picked up one of the curved blades from the table, casually and examined it.

"The name's Mannon," he said, his voice low and sonorous, "I do love it here, among the detritus of your psyche. You have such promise, Falkir. Love and loyalty turned to betrayal, murder and even cannibalism. I commend you your appetite."

"You think you know me?"

"In a way, I know all of you. Or at least, I know what is in your hearts."

"That's a bold statement for someone I've never met or heard of."

"That's true; I haven't been around for a very long time. Before your time, anyhow."

"What do you want with me?"

Mannon turned to me, putting the blade down on the table.

"I need you, Falkir. You and the rest of the Kingdom. I have questions that need answering."

"You would ask me to betray my comrades to you and for what? Some boon? As far as I know, you're just a bad dream."

"Oh, I assure you, I am very real. So is this offer. Let me come to you now and lead me to your friends, or I will hunt down all of you; if you force me to hound you, I won't be so kind when we meet. You have greatness within you, Falkir – you have no idea. We have a lot in common. I thought you might relate to someone who's also been betrayed."

"You are mistaken."

I spun the dagger in my hand and threw it at Mannon's heart. He held up his hand in time and my dagger skewered it. He looked at his hand, fascinated, as a black, viscous substance spilled out and dripped to the earth. He pulled out the dagger. He flexed his wounded hand and I heard his bones creak.

"Will that do for my answer?"

"I will remember this," Mannon replied, "and sometime soon, when I find you and flay the soul of the stupid beast that drove you to your unwise and unkind response, you will reflect, in agony, on your error. Make no mistake: I will find you."

I chuckled as his image disappeared. I walked over to the pool of ichor he left in the dirt and wiped some up with my finger. *If you knew anything, you should have known better than that!* I tasted the ichor on my tongue and the bitterness of it caused me to choke. I cleared my throat and knelt down to where the dog lay.

"Good times, old friend," I said, slapping the corpse, "good times."

The remnants of the dream crumbled and I awoke.

The castle stone was cold beneath my flesh, even under the bundle of furs I used as a bed. Dim, morning light illuminated the room from the small, open window above me. Across from me, the embers of the fire still smoked in the fireplace, doing little to provide warmth in this small room. The dampness of the fortress in Trelaen was constant…I loathed sleeping indoors, but I would not leave Flesh unprotected. *Dogs are loyal, are they not?* I had stayed at her side for the last two weeks since that bastard Mick had strangled her. Since then, she had not awoken, but lay in some sort of coma. She was in a cot a few feet away, her breathing, as always, steady, and strong. But she would not wake up. I rose up from my place on the stones and walked over to her.

The marks from where he strangled her were still there; livid, white marks stood out on her dark skin, a reminder of how dangerous Mick had become. *It was not natural, whatever he did.* I watched as he had let her drop to the table and had recognized the look in his eyes. Mick had become much like me in that moment…cold, distant, and murderous. He had renounced me on that hill not long ago and left me for dead. If it was not for Flesh, I would still be there, frozen on the ice floe where that great cold river had emptied out. It delighted me to think that his heart had turned dark as well, his righteousness burned away in that single act of cold murder. *Although she was not dead, she might as well be.*

I turned around to see if the door to the room was shut. It was, so I turned back to where Flesh lay below me. I pulled back her robe to reveal her naked body beneath and began the daily ritual that had started before she fallen into this sleep that could not be sleep…her sex did not interest me – I had lost the taste for that long ago. Flesh' gift to me stirred in my body in a different way and I felt my canine teeth lengthen. I knelt down and used one sharp tooth to pierce the wound that had served me so well. I bit down and felt the salty tang of her blood splash into my mouth.

"It is so lonely without you," I said, between suckling mouthfuls.

Tears, the last refuge of a long ago broken and damned man, so buried in the past before I was truly myself, spilled down my ruined cheeks to wet her thighs. I stopped feeding and tried to choke back the bitterness I felt. I stood, dressed her wound and restored her dignity. I wiped my mouth and bent low to kiss her. It was always on the ruined side of her face that I kissed, for I knew that it was her distortion that had given me life again.

"He will die by my hand," I whispered, caressing her face, "I swear it to you."

MICK

I shivered in the cold as I appeared again in Tiroj. Everything I beheld was in stark relief, the dark shadows of the trees, flush against the eternal white of winter. Snowflakes flew through the air…it was night here. I pulled my coat closed and looked around. *More time had passed here than I had thought.* The campfire was cold and our bedrolls were gone. Casey was gone. The others had departed as well, or so it seemed. I needed to find all of them. The snow blew around me and I summoned up a fur cloak to keep the cold out. I decided to make my way to the village. Perhaps my friends, or so I hoped they still were, had travelled there to seek shelter.

As I moved along the trail that wound its way through the forest towards the Tiroji village that I had come to know so well, I mulled over my meeting with Father. I didn't know if I could trust him, which seemed to be a strange thought to have about what seemed to be the creator of all things. Considering my situation though, I didn't have much choice. I had been wandering the worlds in order to get some answers about myself and my people, to connect with them and find a place to belong to. Now, I have those answers. I had gone through hell and paid a heavy price, but it would be worth it if Father made good on the deal. *A world of our own…a home.*

I wondered, looking at my corrupted hand, if I would ever see that home; so far, my path had led me on a merry journey of conflict, genocide and painful revelation and I knew in my heart that the worst was still yet to come. The vision that kept me going was of me in a house on a farm, far from the seas and storms, living out eternity in peace with Casey, if she would have me again. Doubt besieged me, calling me a fool and a liar. I pushed it aside. My vision was a small piece of hope, but I had to hang on to something. *I had to.* The snow crunched under my feet and the wind howled at my back, pushing me onward.

I could now see lights in the distance…but they were too close to be the village, which was easily another few kilometers away. I had come too far to be less than cautious at this point, so I drew my sword. I moved off the trail and made my way through the trees toward the source of the lights. It was strange because they appeared to be up in the trees. I could see very little through the snow. I knelt down and grabbed a handful of snow, putting it in my mouth so that no one would see my breath. I crept up slowly to the lights.

I was close to them now and my heart leapt. I could see ropes tethered to the trees and they led up to a ship that hung in the air, lanterns hung along the side of the hull. It was Henri's ship! Of course. I should have guessed that he had brought it along when they had come to me in the camp. A small campfire lingered near where it was tethered. I couldn't see anyone there, or on the deck up above, but I was at a disadvantage from where I was on the ground. They must have decided to sleep in the airship – I couldn't blame them; it was a miserable night. I moved closer to the ship and called out to see if anyone was aboard.

Casey poked her out from above me on the deck.

"Hey, Mick."

I felt the sting of tears in my eyes. I bit my lip, looking up at her from below.

"It's so good to see you," I said.

She looked away from me.

"What's wrong?"

It was then that I felt a strong hand wrap around me from behind and a ghostly sword poked from between my ribs. I struggled. There was a familiar click. I looked up to see that Casey had one of her guns drawn and it was pointed at me.

"Don't move, Mick," she said, "Either Otomo will skewer you, or I'll shoot you before you can take our weapons away."

"What the hell is all this!?"

I watched as Henri joined Casey on the deck, the familiar form of Dakum looming above him as they looked down at me.

"It's all about trust, Mick," Henri said, "and right now, we're running pretty low."

"There's no need for this! Casey?"

She said nothing and kept a tight bead on me.

"Says you," Henri said, "Dakum?"

Dakum stepped forward. His eyes were narrowed and I could feel the power moving in him. I knew what was coming; it would be better than getting impaled, but only slightly. He raised one hand, curled it into a fist and swung it around in a backhand motion. The blow hit me like a cannonball and I felt the world tilt very suddenly as I fell into the snow. Consciousness fled from me as I felt myself being dragged along the snowy ground.

FALKIR

Trelaen was a ruin. Looking over the burned and demolished city, I felt a certain sense of accomplishment. The sky was a dark red and thunder rolled monotonously across the land. The wind whooped up in great gusts, scattering flame and debris across the streets. The mayhem pleased me greatly. Lethia's mysterious item had remained mysterious, though. I had led raids on all of the city's places where Penny indicated, but we still had nothing. I wondered and not for the first time, what exactly we were wasting our time on here…there were other worlds to explore and conquer, to bend to our will and to feed on. The thought of finding where Mick was from and burning and devouring all that he knew and loved was especially appealing. I had promised Flesh that he would die at my hands and I intended to fulfill that wish.

It was another of Lethia's dark moods that brought us all out onto the terrace where I now stood. She had ordered servants to bring her throne out onto the terrace so she could look over Trelaen and plan out our next move. We all knew that at least one or two of the servants would be drained and thrown over the side – it was just her way. I couldn't remember if it was my turn to toss the corpses over or not. Jack and Penny sat to the right of her throne as consultants. Nicholas and I knew very well that she didn't keep us around for our wisdom and intellect. I didn't care, but Nicholas bristled every time. He leaned over the terrace on the railing, brooding in boredom. I fought the urge to stick out my foot and kick him over the side. He seemed to be daring me, but I didn't take the bait. Lethia wouldn't like that.

"What do you mean that you don't hear them talking anymore?" Lethia growled.

"I mean just that, my queen," Penny replied, "the voices that guided me here no longer speak to me. Ever since Mick left, they've become utterly silent."

Lethia sighed and I took note of how Jack's hand had moved to rest close to his jacket pocket where I knew he kept his revolver. Jack's loyalty was always to Penny, no matter what he said or did. It didn't matter; I could disembowel him before he had time to aim. I looked over to Nicholas, who was making a good show of not noticing Jack, or anything for that matter. I knew that look, though. Nick was a lot like my father that way, prone to sudden bursts of anger and brutality that had been hidden by the silent storm of a sullen mood a moment before. I hated Nick for that reason alone.

"Then what use are you to me, or the Kingdom?"

Penny cringed.

"My queen, I must protest. Penny has proved herself to be a valuable member of our group," Jack said.

Jack was on his feet now.

"Her value is whatever I say it is, Jack," Lethia said, "And you would do well to remember your place."

"My place? My place is also whatever I say it is, my queen. Without my power, those beasts of Flesh' would be just mindless monsters, undirected and without purpose. Especially now that she's out of the picture – there's no one else to command your armies, Lethia. Penny will not come to harm as long as I am around and you need me."

I fully expected Lethia to rip Jack's arms off, or that she would ask me to do it, but there was a ring of truth in what Jack said and she knew it. In answer she floated up from her throne, her rage in check and moved over to stand nose to nose with Jack. I noticed Jack sparing a glance to look over at me and I merely drummed my fingers against the hilt of my dagger. Jack smirked and backed down to sit with Penny.

"This posturing is getting us nowhere," he said, "We're tearing at each other because we've lost purpose. Penny and I have been talking and we think the best course of action would be to find Mick and his band."

I gripped the hilt of my dagger.

"I second that."

"The only question is where to start," Lethia said, "Falkir, are you able to—"

"Were there cars in the city?" Nick interrupted, "Because if not, there is one now."

I rose from my seat to join Nick at the rail. He pointed at a blur of motion and a shine of chrome a few hundred metres down the wide boulevard, past a large decorative fountain in the city square. I could see that it was a car and it was headed our way. Our minions, Flesh' monsters and those citizens who had surrendered to us, were scrambling to get out of the way of the rumbling vehicle.

"Perhaps we should adjourn to the hall, my queen?" Jack asked.

"Nonsense," Lethia replied, "Nicholas, if you will?"

I felt the air heat up as Nick crafted the green fire from his hands, a large ball of it dancing on his fingers. He took a moment to give it strength and then hurled it like a shot down the length of the street towards the vehicle. Whatever I have said of Nick, he was a damned good shot. The ball of fire hit the car right in the front, exploding over it and engulfing it in flames. Lethia laughed in delight. A moment later, the car exploded. Nick cracked his knuckles.

"Well, that certainly made my day," he mused.

"Don't pat yourself on the back yet, Nick," Jack said.

I looked over to see that Jack had activated his abilities and was controlling our minions at the scene. Jack had a slightly worried look on his face.

"What is it?" I asked.

"Something just climbed out of the wreckage and it's still coming this way. I'll intercept it."

We were all up now and standing near the railing. I drew my dagger. It was a fifty-foot drop to the street from here, but I could make it; whoever or whatever it was, it wouldn't get to Lethia without going through me. Nick's hands were filling with fire again as well.

"It's tearing them apart! I can't make out what it is – it's all black!" Jack shouted.

As I watched Jack's worried face, I also saw that Penny was staring directly out over the street to where the conflict was taking place. Her face had gone white and she was trembling. She took a step back. Our minions had gathered in a mob and were attacking the intruder. Bodies were being flung in all directions. I moved to stand on the rail.

"We…we need to get out of here," she whispered, "Jack…we need to leave… now!"

"Protect the queen," Jack said, "I can't hold it back…shit!"

The crowd parted like a breaking wave and a humanoid form all in black ran past them.

"Nick! Do it now!" I screamed.

Nick unleashed fire in waves, bathing the figure in green, burning death. It wasn't even slowing down. It hurled something and whatever it was hit Nick in the head. He collapsed to the floor of the terrace. I was about to jump over when the figure itself leaped, clearing the fifty feet or so in one incredible lunge. I struck at it with my dagger as it flew over me, then felt something wet hit me in the chest. I tumbled over to join Nick on the floor. I scrambled to get up as I heard Penny scream.

Jack was down now too and the figure in black stood on top of him, one foot on Jack's neck and the other on his groin. It held the severed limb of one of the wolfmen in one hand. It struck Jack in the head with the limb and then casually tossed the limb over its shoulder. I rushed in, intending to plunge my dagger into its ribs. It grabbed my arm and twisted it around until it was in a tight joint lock. I reached for another knife.

"Now, now," it said, "let's not be hasty here, boy."

The blackness disappeared and the man from my dreams, Mannon, stood before me. His suit was immaculate, his expression calm and detached.

"I told you I would find you, Falkir. Ready to pay the piper?"

MICK

The floorboards above my head creaked as someone paced back and forth. They'd been doing it for the last twenty minutes. My first guess would be Casey, my second Henri. I could've heard the difference if Dakum was pacing and I wouldn't have heard Otomo move around at all. I couldn't see a damned thing…the clever bastards had tightly blindfolded me so I couldn't see things directly to swap into my hands to escape. My hands were shackled behind me, so that was also holding me back. The pacing had been there when I regained consciousness half an hour ago. The murmurs above me had ceased though. I was really hoping that maybe Casey was pleading for me, but how things had been lately between us, it could go either way. I still couldn't believe they had done this.

Sure, I'll be the first one to admit that things between us all had gone pretty strange since I'd lost my marbles a bit back in Trelaen; what I'd done to Flesh, coupled with what Apostos had told us when I'd finally subdued him, probably didn't cast me in a very good light. The past was all Lichonus, though. They couldn't possibly blame me for what he'd done! They didn't know the half of it though…it was essential that I got a chance to get free and talk it out with them. For all I knew, the Kingdom was working toward doing the kind of damage that would obligate Father to move against them. That, of course, would mean that I had failed and the obliteration of all the worlds would soon commence.

It hadn't happened yet, so that was good.

I was sitting cross-legged on the floor, which I could tell was old, treated wood by the musty smell. I could feel the room sway slightly. We were probably on board Henri's ship and I was in some kind of cargo hold. If I remembered correctly from the last time I'd been on board, there were probably a set of stairs less than ten feet away that led up to the crew deck, if only I could get free to use them. I shuffled around, trying to find a more comfortable position, but stopped as a new murmuring sound began in the room…*no…not in the room.*

In my head.

"Mick…" a voice whispered.

What the hell should I do here? It wasn't as if I should reply out loud…I didn't want to give my friends any more reasons to suspect that there's something seriously wrong with me.

…There's nothing wrong with you that isn't wrong with them… the difference is that they haven't gone through the same ordeals that you have. Just think what you want to say…

Oh good, I feel much better about all of this now. I'd ask who the hell you are, but it seems kind of stupid considering that you're in my head.

…True. I've been trying to work my way back to the point that I could contact you ever since Trelaen…

Work your way back? What does that mean?

…Mm. Open your eyes in the blindfold, Mick. I'll try to let you see me…

What—

"Can you see me?"

On the edge of my vision, in what would be one corner of a room if the perspective was right, there was a dark-haired young man with strange grey eyes and dressed in the robes and armour I'd come to associate with Apostos and his brothers sitting in the same way I was. Suddenly, with absolute certainty, I knew him.

Lichonus

…Good. Nice to meet you at last. Then again, I suppose we met a long time ago when Father shoved my broken soul into you…

How is this happening?

…Ah. My theory is that Flesh accidentally knocked me loose and unleashed the darkness in you when she fixed your hand. Before that time, I wasn't really conscious. Since then, I've been gaining strength with the darkness. I figured it was time for a talk…

Well, that's great. You must not be too thrilled about the sword then. It's supposed to be pushing back at the darkness.

…And the darkness pushes back in return. Let's not waste time, Mick. I'm expending a lot of power here to talk to you. There's something you need to know…

So, spill already. I've got things to do here as well.

…Very well. I've been listening to everything since Trelaen, especially when you were with Father. Mick, I think he's lying about what's going on and I also think you're following him far too readily…

What choice do I have? He'll lay waste to everything we know and love unless I do what he asks.

…Yes and be assured that he can do exactly that if he wishes. It's what he's said about how all this happened that bothers me. From what I've been listening to in your mind, you're about to try to convince your friends to help you. You need to be honest with them and not follow everything on blind faith; you were a good little soldier once, Mick and so was I. I know how it is…

What do you know, Lichonus?

…It's what I don't know and don't remember that scares me. I remember being summoned by Father and travelling to him. After that, I remember only the time when I was that berserk, awful thing that killed my brothers and sisters and stained them with darkness. Don't you see? There's nothing in between…

You don't know how you came to be infected with it? Nothing at all?

…No. I first thought that there'd been damage to my essence when Apostos tried to obliterate me with the power Father had given him. However, I remember everything else…why not that?

But Apostos gave me the same breakdown of events and why he did it.

…Apostos only knows what Father tells him. If one of us could be altered, why not all of us?

You're freaking me out now.

…Good! Think about what's going on here, Mick! I…

Lichonus' flickered and disappeared.

Hey! Where did you go?

…Too weak…major drain on my resources…watch out, Mick and be aware of what you're doing and who you serve…I'll try to contact you…

Lichonus?

I waited for a minute. There was no reply. He was gone, or so it seemed.

"Mick."

"Lichonus?" I asked, out loud. Damn it.

"No…it's me Apostos. Where the hell are we?"

I felt my blindfold being untied and before long I was squinting in the dim light of the cargo hold below the cabins. Apostos squatted on the deck beside me, looking around.

"First of all, lower your voice. We're in a bit of trouble now. How did you get here, anyway?"

"Father bonded me to you. I was sent to do your bidding. Thanks so much for that, by the way."

"My pleasure. I just didn't want you pulling any more of your tricks on any of us. The idea of you as my servant works for me, though."

Apostos grinned.

"So why are you tied up in the basement of this dismal place, Mick?"

"Well, apparently my friends don't trust me after what happened in Trelaen and the little tale you talked about when I was Lichonus. They subdued me and tied me up down here."

"Hmm…maybe Casey should have received the sword…"

"Piss off. Untie me; we've got work to do."

Apostos began to untie me. I heard a creaking on the stairs.

"Wait!" I whispered.

Apostos left the ground very abruptly and slammed into the ceiling. Dust drifted down from the rafters as Apostos fell to the floor. Dakum crouched on the stairs, his hand held out, palm down. The ghostly form of Otomo drifted through the floor, became solid and landed on Apostos' back with his sword drawn. Seconds later, Dakum moved down the stairs to allow Henri and Casey to join the crowd.

"Well, well," Henri said, "this certainly adds to the debate, doesn't it?"

I did what I should have done before and swapped the bonds that held me to my left hand and tossed them aside behind my back. Otomo moved slightly, a turn of his sword that would bring it across my neck after delivering the killing blow to Apostos. Well, killing blow in name only, I guess.

I struggled up to a kneeling position.

"Why don't we all just calm down here?"

"You think we're being unreasonable, Mick?"

"Just slightly," I replied, "There's a lot you don't know."

Before Henri could reply, Casey grabbed his shoulder.

"Speak your mind, Mick. We owe you that, I guess," she said.

"Fine. First of all, as much as I'm enjoying it, please get off of Apostos, Otomo."

Otomo spared a glance to look back to Henri. Henri nodded and Otomo moved off. So, that was how it was now. Apostos dusted himself off, cast a murderous glance at Dakum and Otomo and moved to stand beside me, his arms crossed. I stood up and flexed to get the cramped feeling out of my arms and legs.

"Okay, folks," I began, "it's story time…"

FALKIR

With one quick and calculated move, Mannon broke my arm. The sensation was wrenching, but the pain was manageable. I had suffered much in my life, broken bones being low on the list of horrific acts against my body. Without missing a beat, he used my arm as a piston to push me back towards Nicholas' unconscious form. I managed not to fall on top of him. I caught myself and dropped down into a crouch, pulling my arm close to my body. If Jack hadn't been distracted, we could've taken him easy, but now he was too close. I underestimated him. He took a step toward Lethia.

"Who are you, beauty?"

Lethia let her form slip into the white-haired monster and floated upwards, above Mannon. He looked up at her and smiled. I maneuvered around, slowly and put myself between him and the archway, which led to Flesh' unconscious form. He raised one eyebrow at me but made no other move.

"I am Lethia and these are my people," she said, "Your actions against us have sealed your fate."

"Just give me Lichonus or tell me where he is and I will depart with no further harm to your little band."

"I have no idea who that is," she replied.

"You're all making this harder than it has to be," Mannon said, "But perhaps it has to be this way."

She flexed her claws and flew down towards him. He watched her sail in at him and did nothing to stop it. I gave Lethia the best chance I could and threw my four remaining knives at him in a volley at his heart. He raised his arms in defense and the knives plunged into his forearms and shoulders. Lethia grabbed him and lifted him up into the air, her hands seeking his flesh to feed. Black droplets began to fall from them in a light rain from their twisting forms, Mannon's wounds supplying the foul ichor. I could not look away.

Penny grabbed my wrist.

"We have to run, now!"

I shoved her away.

"You pitiful, blind coward! I flee from no one. I will not leave Flesh to this man's tender mercies."

"If you could see what I do…"

She shook her head and turned away.

"Do what you must, Falkir."

Penny moved from me to Jack and wrapped him up in her arms. A second later, they were gone. I had never seen Penny move through worlds before…she was fast. She'd have to be as cowardly and weak as she was. I turned my attention to Lethia and Mannon, who were now far above the battlements; I could barely make them out, but it was obvious that he was putting up a fight. I heard Lethia cry out, which was followed by a peal of awful laughter. I was torn…I didn't want to desert Lethia, but I had to get Flesh out of here before it was too late. I reached down and shook Nicholas.

"Get up, you fool! You're sleeping through the end of the bloody Kingdom!"

Nicholas' head lolled to one side and I could see the blood seeping from a crack in his skull. He opened his eyes, which were now cross-eyed. He was screwed. He grabbed feebly at my arm and I shook him off. His hand fell back onto the terrace floor and stopped moving. *We're screwed and it's my fault for not warning them about Mannon.*

One last, strangled cry issued from far above me. It was Lethia. I looked up to see a huge explosion of green light erupt from them. *What the hell was he doing?* I scrambled to one side as they fell towards the terrace. Mannon landed on his feet. In his arms, he held Lethia's limp form. He had one arm across her shoulders and another at her belly. He looked up at me.

"Where is Lichonus, Falkir?"

Who the hell was that?

"Damned if I know," I said.

He dug his fingers into her stomach.

"How right you are."

Lethia's eyes opened and she screamed as he twisted his fingers. Slowly, tendrils of blackness began to drift up from her body. Mannon opened his mouth and began to suck them in. I stumbled back and away; it was all I could do to get away from him. *Who was the coward now?* Lethia began to wither and empty, her body shriveling as Mannon drank her in. I was out of knives and out of time. I turned and ran through the archway and down the hall towards Flesh.

"What's wrong, boy?" he shouted, " I know you're not squeamish. Don't you want to say goodbye to your queen?"

I turned around and took one step toward him before I stopped myself. *I must not fail her...I must get away!*

Mannon dropped Lethia's shriveled corpse to the floor.

"Like I said before, Falkir, you and I have a lot in common. I doubt most people would understand your need to feed. I do. I am sure, however, that not even your comrades understand why you're so eager to protect the woman who gave you back your life…the real reason, anyway."

"You know nothing of me," I snarled.

My face changed, the rage bubbling up in my gut and igniting my power…the beast was now in control. I cried out in exultation as my maw distended and lengthened to accommodate my marvelous teeth. I felt my form strengthen and bulk up as my muscles grew and my bones creaked. My broken arm re-knit itself and I flexed it into a defiant fist.

"But you will learn!"

Mannon laughed as I bounded forward at him, my claws desiring the sinew of his guts. Whatever bitterness flowed in his veins, I would see how he did without a good portion of it. We met in the middle of the hallway. I cut him across the chest and he grappled with me. He flung me against the wall, stunning me for a second. I responded with an uppercut that slashed at his breast and drew a long cut up his face from his lips to his eyebrows. He giggled as it split open and bled.

It was my turn to throw him around. I grabbed the front of his jacket and tossed him, headfirst, into the opposite wall in a cartwheel, pivoting with the full measure of my strength. He managed to get his arms out to cushion the blow, but his head still impacted directly with the stone. He slid down the wall and slumped to the floor. I moved over to finish him. As I reached down to rip out his throat, he opened his eyes and smiled.

"This was how you found your mother," he murmured, "Dead in a ditch, the waste product of her 'relationship' with your sadistic father. Small wonder that you protect Flesh the way you do; your loyalty is touching. I will demand the same."

"How do you know about that?" I asked, my rage turned to bewilderment.

"I was in your head, Falkir. I know about what you're thinking and the memories that flicker by when you're deep in thought. I know that you're just trying to pay back Flesh for what she gave you, unlike your mother who you can never repay because you were too late to stop her from dying. I can help her, Falkir. I can give Flesh back to you."

I began to transform back. The energy bled out of me. If there was any chance that I could help her…

"Why would you help us? You just murdered Lethia and Nicholas, although him I didn't care for much. Either way, it's strange that you would want to help."

Mannon rose from where he had been slumped over. His wounds began to heal and the ichor stopped flowing. He pulled a handkerchief from inside his jacket and began to wipe the stains from his face and hands.

"First of all," he said, sticking his hands in his pockets, "I don't like power struggles. Your little queen didn't seem like the cooperative type from what I've seen in your head. The guy with the fire pissed me off though; I cracked his skull because of it."

"That doesn't explain your interest in me, or your offer to help Flesh."

"It's pretty simple, Falkir. I need you to help me find Lichonus so I can do what needs to be done and get some payback. If you agree to do that, I'll restore Flesh."

There wasn't much I could do. The bastard was nigh-unkillable and I could see he had been just toying with me. The bastard was good.

"And when you have your revenge?"

His face lit up in a joyful grin.

"After that," he said, "I won't care what happens to any of you. It will all be irrelevant."

"That's great," I replied, my heart filling with doubt.

"Cheer up, Falkir," he said, "Why don't you show me to your girl and we can get started."

MICK

Henri's face was a study in the power of the most outlandish of truths to truly mollify even the most ardent disbeliever. He sat down heavily on one of the barrels next to the stairs and exchanged a glance with Dakum. Casey was still standing and was shaking her head. Otomo silently brooded where he had knelt on the floor while I told them what I had discovered. Apostos looked bored. I understood how he felt…we had to get moving, but it was a lot to absorb for all of them.

"So, if I understand what you're saying correctly," Henri said, "this 'Father' thing created a set of worlds with a bunch of shepherds to watch over them so that it can reach some new level of understanding. We were all like Apostos -- shepherds, until something happened to you and you corrupted and killed some most of us. Apostos and his other brothers stopped you and stuffed us all into new bodies with no memories of what happened. Then, it really gets ugly. Enter the Kingdom and your disfigured hand full of darkness. Father gets pissed and decides to use you to wipe out the Kingdom using a sword he made to do it with, in exchange for a world where we don't have to run anymore."

"Yes, that's right."

I was thinking how odd it was when put so simply. Nothing was simple.

"You forgot the part where Father blows up all creation if Mick fails," Casey murmured.

Henri shrugged.

"Yes, sorry," he said, "And here I thought we had it rough before."

"There's more," I said.

"More? God! Or should I say 'Father'? What else can there be?" Henri exclaimed.

"I don't know if this will help at all, because you might just think I've gone crazy, but here it is: I don't know if we can trust Father."

"That is not crazy, Mick," Otomo said, raising his eyebrows at me, "I do not know if I would trust him either. Considering the power that some of us possess, it would not be unusual if he were one of us, masquerading as a god."

"Do you think that's true, Mick?" Casey asked, coming over to sit by me.

I felt a flutter in my heart as she sat down; I'd been missing her so much and her betrayal had hurt me. Having her this close though, was making it hard for me to say what I had to. I looked away from her to Henri.

"I don't know. Anything's possible, but I doubt Father is one of us. The problem right now is that Lichonus has started speaking to me."

"That is not possible, Mick," Apostos said.

"Many things that I think most of us thought of as impossible are happening regardless of that fact, Apostos," Henri said.

"You fail to understand my meaning," Apostos replied, "I was there when Lichonus was stopped; I stopped him. I was also there when Father took each of my fallen brothers and sisters from their shells and put them inside of what would one day be your souls. Father told us then that the essence of what they were remained, but the memories were lost."

I hoped Lichonus was listening. I had planned on trying to get Apostos to talk about what happened. There was something missing from the whole puzzle – I believed that Lichonus would either catch Apostos in a lie or confirm what he was saying so that I could put my trust in Apostos. I needed people I could trust and Apostos still sat on the fence in my mind, despite what Father did or did not do to put me at ease.

"But why, Apostos? Why preserve the essence of the shepherds?" Casey asked, "Especially the essences of those who turned? No offense, Mick."

"None taken, hon; I'm not Lichonus."

She nodded and looked away from me.

"Father told me that energy cannot truly be destroyed but becomes something else. I assumed he did not want to waste what we were, perhaps make something good come of that tragedy? I truly do not know the reason; it is my purpose to obey," Apostos said.

"Blindly?" Otomo asked.

"I put my trust in him," Apostos said, "it is all he has ever asked of me."

"What if I told you that Lichonus is missing his memories of when he met with Father before he became corrupted, until when he was in the midst of destroying the rest of you, of us?" I asked.

"That makes no sense. Even if Lichonus did survive, it is impossible to know what of him lived and what did not."

This was going to be hard for Apostos, but I had to press him on the point.

"What if I told you that I think the darkness inside those who were corrupted survived and that the memories of the shepherds remained in that darkness? Lichonus said he started coming back with the darkness after Flesh repaired my hand. It's like she used her power to open up the darkness inside me and he came with it. You have to admit that it makes a weird kind of sense, doesn't it?"

Apostos said nothing and turned away from me.

"That's okay, Mick," Henri said, "you're trying to make a dutiful son admit that a parent has made a mistake. I remember walking in my mother with her first lover. It was then that I realized how imperfect parents are…"

I barely was able to grab Apostos before he had his hands on Henri's throat. I looked up to see Dakum put down his one hand, smirk, and nod at me; Henri's guardian angel was always on duty – thankfully. Henri straightened his lapels, grinning smugly.

"Your mother is not the maker of all things! She is not possessed of the power to remake the scope of creation on a whim! Father can do that! He can do that! If you doubt it for a second, I can take you to Lichonus' world – it is a graveyard because Father had to stop the corruption there before it spread. He did it because it was his will – no mistakes were made."

It occurred to me then that maybe Apostos was right; no mistakes were made, which was a much scarier thought than any other to me. I tucked my thoughts away for the moment. There was no point in voicing them right now until I had some time to figure out what the real implications were.

"I know I brought all this up, but I have to admit that we have more pressing matters, don't we?" I said, trying to change the subject.

"I guess we do at that," Henri said, his hand digging in his coat for his lighter.

I swapped it into my hand, winked at Henri and tossed it to him.

"Cheeky bastard," Henri mumbled.

"You have some kind of a plan?" Dakum said, stepping off the stairs and joining us.

"Yeah, but let's sit down and grab something to eat," I replied, "I hate saving the world on an empty stomach."

* * * * *

We adjourned to the dining cabin, which I'd never been in before. It was more luxurious than any mess I'd ever dined at on a ship. The room was long, possibly a third of the deck and had a large oak table in its centre flanked by stools and lit from above by small, iron chandeliers. There were portholes along the side, showing the fall of snow out in Tiroj. Back on the *Golden Maria*, we were rationed tinned beef, rum, and lemon water. And we ate it on our bunks. This was truly something else. Platters of beef, chicken and wild game greeted us when we entered. Jugs of some wonderful-smelling liquor were set onto the table. Then, to my astonishment, fresh fruit made an appearance. I greedily eyed an apple that sat on the top of one bowl. Instantly, it was in my hand. Casey punched me in the arm.

"Ow!"

"Save some for the rest of us, jerk," she said, smirking at me.

"Sorry. Just really hungry."

"Seeing as you can have anything you want if you can visualize it, Mick, what is so appealing about an apple?" Otomo asked, scooping up a clutch of dark grapes for himself from a bowl.

"Visualizing is one thing, but I can't have anything I want; it has to exist in the world I'm on. You wouldn't believe some of the funky things I've ended up with instead of what I hoped would be available," I replied and bit into the apple.

It was delicious and very sweet. I stood there, savoring my foodgasm.

"Good lord, Mick," Henri said, clapping me on the back, "you haven't even had the beef yet. Let's sit down and you can feed the need, so to speak."

We sat down together. Casey sat beside me. Henri sat down at the head of the table with Dakum on his right. Otomo sat beside Apostos across from Casey and me. The odd men out, indeed. We all ate with abandon, save Apostos, of course. I knew I was starving, but I hadn't considered that perhaps my companions were just as hungry. Casey was particularly ravenous. She didn't touch the alcohol – hardly any of us did. We all probably feared what could happen if we used our powers while inebriated. No one spoke as we ate. It was Apostos who first spoke.

"I hope you are all enjoying the meal. The worlds are sitting on the edge of a knife while you digest."

"And here I had hoped to digest in peace," Otomo said.

I snatched up a glass of wine and stood up from the table. I moved over to the nearest porthole and began to sip at it. I saw Apostos raising his eyebrows. He got up from the table and moved to join me. I pretended not to notice.

"Did you not hear me, Mick?" he said in a hoarse whisper, "Trelaen is probably in the middle of a fairly decent apocalypse and you lot are having high tea!"

I grabbed him by the shoulder and pulled him close.

"Get Jack and Penny and bring them here. Can you do that?"

"Of course. Father did not restrict my powers entirely…the Kingdom is still fair game. But why would that help?"

"Don't worry about it. Bring them here as quickly as you can."

"As you wish."

Apostos abruptly disappeared. I laughed at myself a little as a small rush of power welled up in me. We were all servants to something now.

"What the hell?" Henri shouted.

I turned to see Henri, Dakum and Casey on their feet. Otomo was sitting very calmly at the table, his hands out in front of him.

"There are two more guests coming for dinner, Henri," I said, "Can you handle that?"

"This is still my ship, Mick," Henri said, "I say who comes on board and who doesn't. Where did Apostos go?"

I exerted my power, summoning the rope that I had been tied up with in the hold.

"To grab us a tactical advantage," I said to Henri, "Who tied me up anyway?"

Casey got up and grabbed the rope from my hand.

"That would be me," she said, "I'm good with knots."

"Oh, the possibilities," I replied.

She slapped me in the chest with the rope and pointed it at my face.

"You're not out of the doghouse yet, Mick," she said.

She looked at me and sighed.

"Who the hell am I tying up?"

"That depends on Otomo," I replied.

"What depends on me?" he asked.

I turned to him and held out my hand.

"I need your sword. I don't want to have to take it from you, but I will if I have to. Please hand it over."

"I will do no such thing," he said, standing up.

"What do you need his sword for?" Dakum asked.

"Insurance," I said, tuning up some energy to summon Otomo's sword to me if it came to that.

"Against what?" Henri asked, reaching into his coat pocket.

"I would imagine that Mick doesn't want him to chop my head off," Jack croaked, suddenly behind me.

They had arrived. I swapped Otomo's sword into my hand and dove forward as he sprang up and across the table, his fists no doubt raised to deliver destruction on Jack. He went ghostly and I passed through him. Damn it! I was hoping to avoid this. I spun around in time to see Otomo get smashed out of the air by a bolt of green lightning. It actually hit him! I looked back to see Henri holding a smoking, ornate-looking gun that glowed with power. He spun it on one finger and put it back inside his coat.

"Necessity is the mother of invention, Mick," he said, "I'll bet you're glad you came quietly before, aren't you?"

FALKIR

Mannon had given Flesh back to me and restored her to consciousness. He had grinned at me as he had lifted her robes before reviving her and saw the marks from my feeding. He had healed those too. I said nothing, then. What could I say? I stayed with her as she woke to the screams of Mannon draining the life out of Nicholas on the terrace.

"Falkir…what happened?" she whispered, her eyes black and far away.

"I have damned us both, love," I said, taking her hand.

She looked up at me now. Did she remember what I was doing to her…could she? She tightened her grip on my hand.

"What do you mean? Who is that screaming?"

"Nicholas," I said, "He's dying."

She started to rise, but I gently guided her back down.

"Nothing I know of can stop that from happening," I told her, "As for the other thing, you'll see what I mean soon enough."

I took her into the dining hall and made her eat something. The servants, the ones she had made, hung about her like lost children. She urged them to back off and let me help her. Her attention was drawn constantly to the hall that led to the terrace. I tried to keep it out of my mind as I tended to her.

"Who is out there, Falkir? I know you're trying not to think about it. When I awoke, I sensed something moving close…something terrible."

I knelt in front of her, dreading that I would have to admit my failure and the weight of my disgrace.

"If you love me, tell me what is going on," she said.

"Lethia is dead, along with Nicholas," I told her, "Jack and Penny have fled as well. We are alone."

She frowned and reached out to stroke the back of my head, running her fingers through my hair. A pair of heavy footsteps sounded from the hall and Flesh raised her gaze to the doorway as Mannon entered the dining hall. I turned around, watching him as he stood there, his hands folded in front of him formally, like some kind of servant awaiting our pleasure. He mocked us with the hold he had over us.

"Feeling better, are we?" he asked her, moving towards us.

I stood up and put myself in between them.

"Whoa there, lover boy," he said, "I just want to sit down and have a conversation with you both.

There's no need to be hostile. No point, either, but I understand."

"Who are you?" Flesh asked.

"My name is Mannon," he said, "and I'm the reason that you're back walking and talking."

He nudged past me and sat down in a chair next to her. I wished I had the strength to fight him, but I had tried that already and failed. I had a feeling he was even stronger now, after Nicholas. To defy him now would be death for the both of us.

"Do you believe you are owed something for it?"

"All of you owe me. The question you should be asking is: what do I want?"

I pushed Flesh' minions out of the way and sat down beside her.

"You told me before that you know us and now you're saying that we owe you…who are you to us?"

"I'm the reason that you are how you are," he said, "The darkness in you is mine, or mine on loan, so to speak. Without me, you'd be as weak as those you fight against."

A horrible feeling of coming into the story halfway through entered my mind. I thought of Apostos and what Mick had told me, so long ago now, about what he believed was going on. *What did he know that we don't?* We had the oracle, damn it! Now, Jack and Penny were gone and the last thing they suggested was going to find Mick.

"What do you know of them?"

"Only what I could learn from being in your head. I have Lethia's and Nicholas' memories now too. The one called Apostos intrigues me. He resembles someone I once knew."

"Who is the one you're looking for, this Lichonus?"

Mannon looked up at me and his eyes became huge and black.

"He is the key to my plans here, my greatest ally. Our greatest ally, I suppose now that I am the leader of the Kingdom. I need to find which of you that he is inside."

Inside?

"What do you mean? Is that why you killed Lethia and Nicholas?" Flesh asked.

"Not exactly."

He stood up and walked away from us towards the terrace.

"Follow me, the both of you."

It didn't seem like we had a choice. I took Flesh' arm as we walked together out to the terrace. We found Mannon standing near the railing, looking out over the city. The storm boiled above us, the winds stronger now as clouds streamed and burned across the sky. Mannon pointed up at them.

"What is happening there?"

"From what we understand, the longer we stay in one place and use our powers, the world starts to distort and go mad. Our wretched counterparts seem to think that we don't belong anywhere. We believe that the worlds are ours to do with as we wish," Flesh explained.

Mannon laughed loud and long, leaning on the rail for support.

"You truly are my children," he said, taking a breath.

"What do you want with us, Mannon?" I asked.

"You're going to help me send a message," he said, "A message that those who are looking for it will understand."

He rubbed his chin with one hand, frowning slightly as he looked back over the city.

"How do we do that?"

"Use your minions to round up as many of the population as there are left and drive them into the courtyard below. That will do for a start."

MICK

We moved Jack and Penny down into the very hold where I had been tied up. They went pretty quietly. Jack really didn't have much choice in the matter, as he looked like he ended up second best in a fight with a baseball bat. I could see that Penny had wrapped a bandage around his chest and there were numerous small wounds on his scalp and face where fresh bruises and abrasions bloomed like flowers. I added that to the list of topics for discussion. As a courtesy, we didn't tie them up. I set Apostos to watching them while they reclined on the benches in the hold. Penny looked very shaky as she tried to make Jack comfortable. I stood there with Apostos, keeping watch on them as Casey came down, dressed in jeans, a blousy shirt, and her cowboy hat. Her pistols hung across her hips and her hands were splayed across the belts. She walked over to me and leaned in.

"Have they said anything yet?"

"I haven't started asking any questions," I replied, "How's Otomo?"

"Pissed off. He's already threatening to leave if we let them stay. What's your play here?"

I pulled her over, out of ear shot.

"They know the current state of affairs with the Kingdom and we need to know what they know before we hit them. Besides, they're not on my hit list, according to Father, so I figure if they're out of the way, it'll be easier."

"You really think they'll tell us anything?"

"Jack won't. He's probably still loyal. Penny, though…looks pretty shook up. Something's happened."

Casey nodded and looked over at the pair where they lay on one of the benches. She drummed her fingers and I could hear the gears turning.

"How are you with all of this?"

"You're making some pretty fast moves, Mick," she said, taking my arm, "Henri's nervous and I don't blame him."

"That's not really what I was asking," I said, taking up her other hand in mine.

"You want to know if you can trust me not to shoot Jack, or if I trust you?"

"Both, really."

"What we did to you Mick, we had to…I'm sorry for not coming to your defense…does that answer your questions?"

I slipped my arms around her and held her.

"I don't want to lose you to this war," I whispered.

"You won't," she said, "Do you remember what I said before Father took you away?"

I remembered that she had taken hold of me when Father had arrived to help Apostos. She had shouted something that I couldn't hear above the thunder that Father had brought with him. I had a pretty good idea of what she said though.

"I love you too," I said.

I never really said it to anyone before…or meant it.

She stood there with me and smiled. She kissed me. I remembered the bed of flowers under a desert sky and I kissed her back, suddenly wishing that I didn't have the weight of worlds on my back and that I could put down this sword. I gave her one last squeeze before letting go.

"Tell Henri that I'll be up as soon as I've talked to these two," I said.

"He'll want to hear everything," she said, "Come find me when you're done."

I nodded and she headed up the stairs.

I turned back to see Penny staring at me, a look of wonder on her face. Jack was breathing very slowly and he stared at the bulkhead.

"What is that you have on your back, Mick?" she asked.

"You've been brought here to answer questions, Penny, not to ask them. Are you talking about the sword?"

"You know I am, Mick; don't be so coy. What I told you about the whispers that I was hearing and your dreams…what you have there is the answer to them all."

The last time I talked with Penny was at the castle in Trelaen where I was being held prisoner. She had told me that my dreams were the key to finding what Lethia was looking for. As it turned out, my dreams were being used by Father to prepare me for taking up the sword. I wondered if Father had been whispering to Penny as well…

"Enough about all of that for now," I said, walking up and sitting down beside them, "What you're going to tell me is what you and the rest of the Kingdom have been up to and where they are now."

"Screw yourself, Mick," Jack whispered, hoarsely, "We're not telling you a damn thing."

"That's not really an option for you at the moment. The hour is getting late and the Kingdom is pushing the buttons of a very powerful being that will wipe the worlds clean of all life, including us, if you're not stopped. I need to know where to find the rest of your people."

"You think that we're going to trust you after what you did to Flesh?" Jack said, pushing himself up to look at me.

Penny scolded him and tried to make him lie back down.

"You will because it's in your best interests. Let's start with who beat the crap out of you, Jack."

"Falkir," he muttered, grinning.

"You're lying," I said, "If you'd gotten in a fight with Falkir, you'd have your guts on your shoes, or your throat torn out. Try again."

"It was someone called Mannon," Penny whispered.

"Shut up, Penny, for all our sakes," Jack moaned.

At the mention of the name, I felt something inside me twitch. My ruined hand tightened into a fist.

"Who the hell is that?" I asked.

"He took out Falkir and Nicholas without much effort and did this to Jack before he and Lethia got into it. I got us out of there before things got worse."

"We shouldn't have left them," Jack growled.

"It was only a matter of time before Lethia killed us both, Jack and you know it," Penny said.

It was pretty clear that things had deteriorated for them in the Kingdom and maybe Lethia was too much of an egomaniac to let Jack have so much power. This new threat seemed to have come from nowhere and broken their circle pretty easily. That simple fact made me curious about his loyalties.

"What did he want?" I asked, "I doubt something powerful enough to take all of you out like that would've done so without a purpose."

Penny looked back and forth between us. Finally, she spoke.

"He wanted to know where to find someone called Lichonus," she said, looking directly at me.

Apostos turned his head toward Penny. I tried not to show any reaction.

"It's okay, Mick," she continued, "I know that you know who he is and where he is. The whispers spoke of him once as the fallen son. They used your name interchangeably with his. Have I said enough yet?"

"Not yet. Tell me more about Mannon," I said.

"I told you that I see those who have power, Mick. I see those like us as outlines, brimming with green fire. I see Apostos as a silvery shadow. What I saw when I looked at Mannon was something different, something terrible…it was worse than being blind. I don't know what he looks like to see him as you do, but to me he is huge, a giant black tornado that tore through Trelaen and became a fiery black shadow when it touched down. If he's after you, you better start running now."

"Why do you think he's after me?"

Penny got up from where she sat and put her hand on my shoulder.

"When I look at you, I can see something writhing inside you," she said, "It looks like a writhing silver shadow not unlike yours, Apostos. Something's hiding inside you, Mick. I think we both know what it's hiding from now, don't we?"

"I think running is an especially good idea," Jack said, getting up from the bench, "And if you are what he's looking for, I'd also like to get the hell away from you, if you don't mind."

I moved close enough to nearly be face to face with Jack. He grinned, his bruised and scraped-up face making him wince slightly in the act. I straightened his tie and brushed at his right shoulder.

"The sad thing, Jack, is that if I win and I can stop your companions from screwing up the worlds, you and I will breathe the same air together, living on one world."

"That sounds like a lousy deal," he said, "Whose idea was that?"

"Mine. It was part of the bargain Father offered me," I replied, "He also told me that I didn't have to kill either of you to make that happen, so be grateful."

Jack backed off and sat back down on the bench. I turned back to Apostos.

"We need to talk. Give these two some breathing room for a bit."

Apostos nodded and followed me up the stairs.

"There are worse places to be, you two," I shouted down the stairs, "Don't give me a reason to send you to them."

* * * * *

We stood in the small room above the hold. There were two upholstered chairs by a small wood stove that was bolted to the floor. I reached into a basket beside the stove which was filled with kindling and threw a couple pieces in to warm the place up. I knew that Apostos couldn't have cared less, but I was tired of freezing my arse off on Tiroj. I sat down in the chair closest to the stove and motioned for him to sit down. Apostos eased himself down into the other chair and tapped his fingers on the arms.

Since we had met, Apostos had become increasingly more human. He was much less like a god now and more like one of us. Bad company, maybe. He had certainly cut down on the pretensions since our little confrontation before Father came to enlighten me. He no longer wore the armour and his hair was tied back to gather in the folds of his hooded tabard. In truth, he looked no more out of place than we ever did. Hell, I still wore a fur cloak over a linen shirt crisscrossed with straps from scabbards and smelling vaguely of some very hard travelling.

"Tick-tock, Mick," he muttered.

"I know. I need to straighten some things out with you before we charge into Trelaen, though."

"What would those be?"

"Before we really get into it, I'd like to remind you that you're in my service now and I expect some answers. In other words, no more playing coy."

"I agree. The hour is getting late."

"The first thing I need to know is: who is Mannon?"

He shook his head, furrowed his brow.

"I don't know. I have the oddest feeling that I should know, but as soon as I try to grasp at that notion, it disappears."

"Do you think Father knows?"

"If he does, he has never told me of him."

I opened the stove and threw in another piece of kindling. I sifted the coals around with an iron poker.

"I'm beginning to feel as if there's a lot that he knows that he never told any of you," I said, "The fact that Penny can see what you told me was impossible, twisting away inside me, leads me to believe that everything is either going way off his grand plan, or working exactly the way he wants it to."

"Is it not enough that he is offering your people a world to live on? Why question that? Why interfere with the grand scheme if it's to your benefit?"

"I know that this is going to be hard for you to understand, because you're not human, but most of us live with a lot of uncertainty about what's real and what's not. My people are still human, no matter what the portion of Father's power that he instilled in us has allowed us to do. Right now, I'm about to lead them into battle against our own people for the chance to co-exist. That's all messed up on its own. Add the fact that I seem to have a lively ghost running around inside my head sowing doubt about the creator of the universe and then add into the mix a new player that doesn't like our enemies much but seems very dangerous on his own. I have a lot of questions right now, Apostos and no one seems to know the answers. That scares me."

"Most of your worrying is pointless though," he replied, "because no matter what you decide to do, Father will carry out what he has promised and start again from ground zero. He has done it before."

Arguing with Apostos about the trustworthiness of our divine creator seemed pointless; I could not shake the foundations of his faith with my misgivings. It was best that I just move on to the hard part.

"There's something I need you to do, Apostos. It's going to be dangerous, but it has to be done so that the attack will succeed."

He rose from his chair.

"I know what you want, Mick. It has been written on your face since Penny told you. You need to know about Mannon and I am your best chance of spying on him and coming back in one piece."

"And so?"

"It is your will and so I will take it as Fathers own."

"Even though he may be as dangerous as the darkness in me was to you?"

"Mick, even if something does happen to me, I have faith that Father will try to help me or recover me if I am damaged or destroyed in his service. I will do as you ask."

"I wish I had your reassurances," I said, "Thank you for what you're going to do. Can you leave in an hour or so? I'll wait for as long as I can before we attack so you can report back."

"As you wish. What about Jack and Penny? Surely you are not taking them with you," he said.

"Oh, I have someone in mind that can make sure they stay put."

"Is he reliable?"

If he wasn't drunk, out on a hunt, or having relations, sure.

"Of course."

Apostos raised one eyebrow and then moved back downstairs to check on Jack and Penny. I watched him go…would I see him again? It was strange to feel compassion for him, considering our history of conflict and mutual dislike, but I guess it just confirmed that I was still operating on a human level. That was good and not so good. On one hand, I was comforted by the fact that my soul was still intact despite the corruption in my body, but I also dreaded its burden.

I hated the weight of having so much on my shoulders and holding the lives of my friends in my hands. On the *Maria*, my old ship from before I awakened to this new life, I had the same duties and I faced them with the same disdain. I wished that I could bury my heart for safe keeping for the next day or so and come back for it after the horror was done with me. I knew, though, that my wish was merely a whisper in the whirlwind; it was one small sound in the cacophony of screaming that was the unending background score for this universe.

FALKIR

The remaining people of Trelaen, great and small, were huddled into the square around the fountain below. Nobles huddled in groups with bakers, policemen and even prostitutes. I suspected the nobles knew them well…whores really made the bridge in a community. Sex was one great equalizer and here was another: fear. I had led Flesh's creations in rounding them up. Some had come quietly, while others had resisted. Many ended up on the end of my claws. I had thought about eating one or two of them, but Mannon's instructions had been specific. Terrifying them would come later, he said. Later was, most definitely, now.

Our wolves circled them, keeping them in line. Flesh and I stood together on the terrace, waiting as Mannon reduced a couple of our human servants inside to rotting husks. He was much like Lethia…I doubted very much that a human population would have supported both of them and their appetites for long, let alone myself as well. The screams of surprise and horror died down inside and the new king walked out to join us.

Mannon always looked the same, minus splotches of gore and such. Today, he looked like an older version of Jack in a more expensive suit. He was dark-haired and tanned, in a black suit and a black shirt with a black tie. It all went well with his thoughts and actions. His teeth were very white and he smiled at us as he approached; he grinned even more as he looked out over the huddled masses below.

"This is going to be one of those moments when you look back and say, 'wow, I was there when that happened,' or maybe you just scream and go catatonic. Either way, I'd say it's going to be bloody unforgettable, wouldn't you say?"

I hated when he tried to buddy up, but I was afraid he'd beat Flesh, or drain her, so I didn't tear out his bloody throat.

"Whatever you say," I muttered.

"Exactly," he said, stepping up to the railing.

"Quiet them down; I want to address them."

I howled out to the crowd and the other animals, the others who had been improved by Flesh, answered me in a single, deafening roar. In the seconds that passed after, no one below spoke, save for a few children that had awoken and were crying. The natural human inclination, to fear the sound of a predator, held them in thrall. This was usually when the predator came out of the brush and ate its prey. Mannon cleared his throat.

"Citizens of Trelaen, I welcome you to this impromptu meeting. For some of you, what I'm about to say won't come as much of a surprise. For others, it just might scare you down to your soul. I have no idea what that's like, as I have no soul, but I'd imagine it must be terrible. I digress...I wanted to tell you, first of all, that there's no one watching out for you now; there's no imaginary heavenly being readied to help you if you fall, or to pick you up after. He, She, or It...sorry. You're praying to an empty sky, folks. The good news is that there's no punishment for all the things you do...killing each other, fucking each other, fucking your neighbor's children, sharpening a blade with full intention of beheading someone, coveting your neighbor's donkey and so on...no consequences. The only thing you can expect is a single sound,"

Mannon clapped, vigorously and smiled.

"I applaud the things you do. You have proved, time and time again, that I was right about what you were and what you're good for, from the very beginning. The bad news is that there's no one to stop people like me from doing exactly what I want. I think a demonstration is in order."

Mannon stepped over to Flesh and put his arms around her from behind. He looked over at me, his gaze warning me to stay away.

"Let's make something beautiful together," he said.

He reached up under her robes and smoothed over her skin. She looked over at me as he began to caress her...something started moving from him to her! I moved to try and separate them.

"I just need her for a moment, lover-boy," he said, "Interfere again and I'll suck her dry and you can go hump her husk. Does that sound good to you?"

"I may be a monster," I growled, "But it is you who are truly monstrous."

"You ain't seen nothin' yet," he replied.

He thrust at Flesh and she screamed out.

"Breath it out, girl," Mannon said, his hands writhing over her body.

Flesh shrieked and her eyes flared green in two tiny sunbursts.

Her mouth opened and a cloud of blackness flowed out. It was liquid smoke, black as night and alive with a sinister flow. It made its way down into the throng of citizens in the square, like a shark swimming in the air. There was a mass of panic and screaming as people tried to get away. There was nothing that could be done from up here, even if I cared to. I saw a couple of the wolves get trampled, along with a couple of older folk who didn't move fast enough, but it was too late for anyone to escape.

Screams began to issue from underneath he blanket of darkness.

Mannon lowered Flesh onto a chair and snapped his fingers. One of the remaining human servants brought out wine and filled glasses on the table. Mannon scooped up one and handed it to me. I turned away from it. He shrugged and took a sip from it.

"Magic time," he said, nodding at the crowd below.

The sounds of screaming changed to bestial snarling. As the cloud dissipated, no men and women remained beneath its sway. Instead, black-skinned humanoids covered with dark, sticky fur struggled in a mess of bodily fluids to get to their feet. I could see claws and teeth as white as Mannon's protrude from the creatures and their eyes were pupil-less and black. Even the children were thus transformed; they were smaller versions of the abominations.

As I watched, a band of the larger ones jumped a few of those who were still human, or in the middle of transforming and tore them apart in a flurry of glee and evisceration. Deep inside, I could feel revulsion towards them...there was nothing redeemable about them at all. They finished with the corpses and joined the rest of their ilk in a herd that started to move back into the city.

"This is a much more honest representation of humanity, don't you think?" Mannon asked me, taking the last sip of his wine, "Cutting through all the sentiment and self-delusion, right to the meat of what they really are."

I moved over to where Flesh lay in the chair and picked her up in my arms. Her breathing was shallow and she was pale.

"I don't give a damn," I replied, "Will Flesh recover from what you've done?"

"Yes, your little playmate will be fine, Falkir," he said, "I just needed to use her as a lens for my power for a moment."

"D<u>on't</u> go far," he said.

He took another glass from the table and held up a toast to the sky.

"Did you like that, you bastard? Did you see what I did to your worthies? Chew on that and remember who fed it to you," he screamed and drained the glass.

"I thought you said that there's no one up there," I said, choosing my words carefully.

"No one who gives a shit," he said, before spitting on the earth.

MICK

We stood together, maybe for the last time, below Henri's ship in our little makeshift camp. Henri was fiddling with some kind of wiring in a device he had in a box, pausing every once in a while to infuse it with power. Dakum was struggling to put on some kind of bronze armour that Henri had put together for him. We had agreed that we had to minimize the amount of contact we would have with the Kingdom and Henri had begun putting together weapons and equipment to supplement our powers for the upcoming battle. He hadn't had much notice, so what he was putting together was pretty amazing; I forgot how little of Henri's talent is inherent in his powers and how much of what he did was due to his intellect.

Casey was practicing drawing her pistols under a heavy brown cloak that had been her own before Henri had modified it. Instead of a simple riding cloak, there were now lightweight plates built into it that came together to form an armoured apron while she was laying down fire. I walked over to her.

"You think it'll work?"

"Me being able to draw, fire and reload, with an extra ten pounds on my damn arms, or the whole thing?"

"Smart-ass."

She smiled, undid the fasteners, and stretched her shoulders.

"Always happy to be of service," she said, tipping her hat, "Any sign of Apostos?"

"Not a whisper," I said.

I tried to shove the guilt down further into my gut.

"That's no good, Mick."

"I know. This might end up being a rescue mission in addition to all the other bloody things we've got to do."

"You said you'd handle Mannon," she reminded me, frowning, "How the hell are you going to do that if you don't know jack 'bout him?"

"I had the same question, Mick," Henri said, helping Dakum attach his breastplate.

I moved over to Dakum and stood on the opposite side of where Henri was. He nodded at the leather strapping. Dakum rolled his eyes as we both heaved on the straps and secured them into the catches on the back-plate. I knocked my fist against the breastplate, earning a tough grimace from Dakum. We stood back to have a look.

"I'll take out Mannon, if it comes to that," I said, hoping I sounded more confident than I felt, "If he's as corrupted and dark as Penny describes, then I should be able to hurt him."

"You think she's telling the truth?" Henri said, "Maybe it's a trap."

"I doubt it," I said, "But we should have some kind of fallback position just in case…maybe somewhere we haven't congregated before?"

"Bersingholt is a good place. It's a resort on the world where I come from," Henri replied, "My parents have a cottage there that would suffice."

"I never would've pegged you as a rich boy," Casey said and stuck out her tongue.

Henri struck a haughty pose, inclining his neck and pulling out the ruffles around his cuffs.

"Some of us have standards," he sniffed.

"I used to think I did," Dakum said.

We all looked up sharply at him. Casey giggled. Henri gasped and pouted.

"Bitch," he said, turning his pout into a smirk.

"Indeed," Dakum said.

We all laughed. Dakum spoke rarely and for him to crack a joke it was nearly unheard of. There might be a hell of a lot less for a while, depending on how things played out. Our laughter died down as Otomo walked into the camp from wherever he had buggered off to lick his wounds after his attempt to get to Jack. He glared at Henri and stepped over to stand in front of me. Henri moved to speak, but Otomo raised his hand in his direction.

"Do you understand why I did it yet?" I asked him.

"Yes."

"So, what are you going to do now?"

"I will fulfill my obligation to you and to Apostos. I will help you in the coming battle. After that, whether Jack is around or not, I am parting ways."

"That's completely ridiculous," Henri blurted, "If it helps, I apologize for shooting you, but—"

"What you did was dishonorable. A trick. You denied me the chance to correct my action and took it upon yourself to stop me without consideration. That, I cannot forgive."

"Who gives a damn about honour? Things are getting a little serious for such formalities."

"It was the way my people lived," Otomo said, "And I am all that is left of that way of life. I intend to preserve it, no matter the cost."

Henri threw his arms up and stomped off towards the box he had been working on.

I understood, somewhat, how Otomo felt, but I couldn't let him go so easily, even after the incident where he cut off my hand. I was feeling generous, I suppose.

"What happens when we all live on one planet together? Are you going to just stay off by yourself?" I asked him.

"That has not happened yet and I have my doubts that it will."

"Well, aren't you a cheery son of a bitch," I growled, "What happens, here and now, if we don't win and Mannon, or one of the others, decides to try and take you out? You'll be on your own!"

"Then I will die the way I have lived," Otomo said. He walked away from us, back into the forest.

"He's right, I guess" Casey said.

"What do you mean?"

"Well, if we do get the chance to live together, we're gonna to have to set some rules about how we go about our business. Livin' like this is okay, but don't we all want somethin' real? Isn't that what were fightin' for here?"

"Yeah, I guess that's true," I replied, "I just don't know if I'd die on principle, or if I'd try to survive as long as I could to get back to what matters."

"Or who?" Henri asked, from his position, kneeling over the box.

"Or who," I said, looking over at Casey.

She looked back at me and even blushed a little. She looked away, tipping her hat down to hide her smile.

"Aren't you two just the cutest," Henri mused, not looking up.

"It personally makes me throw up a little in my mouth," said Jack's voice, from up above.

I went for my sword and I saw Casey redress her pistols to follow the sound.

Jack stood on the deck of the ship, his hands in his jacket pockets. Penny was hugging his arm for warmth. It was not snowing right now, but it was still plenty cold. We had the fire down here, but the decks of the ship were largely unprotected from the elements.

"Don't move, asshole," Casey said.

Jack waved at us with his free arm, grinning like an idiot. He was lucky that Casey didn't blow his head off.

"Simmi!" I yelled up at the ship.

Simmi poked his head over the rail.

"Yeh?"

I eased up and Casey holstered her guns.

"Everything okay up there?"

"Okey, yeh. We play cards up here, meyheps," he said, "Down there, very tight. No good."

Simmi always hated indoors unless there was drinking involved. I had made him promise not to drink while he guarded those two, but I had no illusions about his disdain for small spaces.

"Fair enough. Behave, you two," I said, giving Jack a threatening glare.

"No problem," Jack replied, "You'll most likely be dead soon at Mannon's hands, so I really don't see that we have to lift a finger."

"We'll see about that," I replied.

FALKIR

I stood on the parapet and watched him come.

Apostos walked very calmly and deliberately up the street that led to the castle, his eyes fixed directly ahead on the front gate. The wind howled around him, sending up whirls of trash and debris that wound strangely around him as he approached. Thunder rolled overhead and lightning struck somewhere in the distance. Mannon's new people started crawling out of the ruins, giving Apostos a look as well. Well, they were sniffing the air to decide if he would be good to eat, but he had their attention, all the same. I sat down on the small stone lip at the front of the parapet and pulled out my bow from my rucksack. It gleamed with the grease that I lined the bag with. I strung it, glancing back and forth between the task and my target. I pulled an arrow from the quiver slung at my side and notched it. From what Mick said, the bastard was almost invulnerable…now that I think about it, he could be lying. Let's see.

I raised my bow and loosed an arrow at Apostos' head.

Faster than I ever imagined a person could be, he raised his hand at the last second and the arrow broke on it, shattering like it hit a brick wall. He seemed to take no more notice of me than that. His eyes never wavered. I drew another arrow and waited. Two of Mannon's people jumped him as he passed the fountain, leaping up from their hiding places. They got within five feet. I loosed my arrow, hoping to distract him so they could go to work on him. No such luck. The arrow was smashed. The attackers…caught fire and burned to ash like they kissed the sun. They collapsed into little piles.

He kept on coming. I was about to leap down at him when he looked up at me and shook his head.

"You are such a profound disappointment," he said.

"I've heard that before," I said.

Judgmental bastard: it added a new dimension to my hate for him.

"I have no doubt about that," he said, smashing his way through the gate.

The wooden portcullis blew outward. I heard pieces of it clatter to the cobblestones. I dropped down from the parapet, leaving my bow on the stones. I turned toward the entrance and pulled out a pair of daggers. He was still walking, deliberately, into the castle. He was approaching the door that led to the outer hall when it opened, spilling wolfmen out into the corridor. They snarled at him, baring their claws and teeth. His pace never slowed. He ploughed into them, crushing one like he was nothing. Enough of this! I sprinted forward to join in the fray. I hoped I was quick enough.

I felt myself being lifted up by the throat as I closed with him. I was being dangled in the air while he killed the rest of them with crushing blows from his other hand and a couple well-placed kicks that were punctuated by the crunching of their bones. I stabbed at his arm repeatedly, but his wounds did not bleed. Mick was telling the truth about Apostos. I was useless against him.

He finished with the wolfmen and stepped through their broken remains to the door.

"Perhaps you are of some use to me after all," he said.

He threw me through the door. Of all the indignities! I felt my shoulder separate as I impacted with it. It was all just meat. My pride ached and this prick would pay the weight for his insults! I landed, transforming into my savage alter-ego. My muscles bulged and my hands lengthening into savage claws. I screamed, the sound turning into a howl as my face cracked, distorting as it became a toothy maw. I would tear his throat out and eat whatever would fit between my jaws! He watched, bemused, as I bounded forward to rip him apart.

"You never learn, Falkir and that is your singular weakness."

His fist came down like a hammer. I slipped underneath it and grabbed for his throat. I was faster in this form and almost had him! His other hand batted my claws away and he delivered a blow to my jaw that staggered me. He was so damn strong…

"You…have…been…a…very…bad…dog!" he said, punctuating each word with a murderous axe-handled blow.

I sank to the ground, my shoulders, neck, and back twitching with pain. This was too much, even for me. Screw you Mannon…you can deal with this prick. I lay there for a moment. Then I felt Apostos grab one of my legs – he was pulling me! I tried to right myself, but he kept on hitting me, the bastard!

* * * * *

A few minutes and a humiliating duration on the ground later, he kicked open the doors to our little meeting hall. Flesh jumped up from the couch she sat upon, her hand going to the sickle that she kept at her side. Mannon only looked up from where he sat at the dining table; he displayed no sense of shock or surprise.

"Does this belong to you?" Apostos said, slinging my mostly limp form from the hall's stone floor to a chair.

"He does, yes," Mannon replied, studying his fingernails.

"What do you want, Mannon?"

Interesting…

"Really? No 'how was the big nothing, Mannon?' or 'long time, no see'? I'm thoroughly disappointed, brother."

Apostos moved over to the table and sat down.

"I am no brother of yours," he said, "Try again."

"Well, well. I must say, I'm honoured," Mannon said, standing up and taking a bow, "You've finally decided to show up. All I had to do was make a mockery of your little pet projects and you come running."

"I am not here to trade barbs with you. We both know our history and who we are. I ask again, what do you want?"

Mannon moved over to Apostos' side and dropped onto his knees. He put his hands together, as if he was to prayer.

"Oh, I'm down here, lord, wicked sinner that I am, pleading for the chance to mend fences, get right with the savior and such…maybe even lay a saint?"

Apostos grabbed him by the collar of his jacket and pulled him close.

"You are an abomination," he whispered, through gritted teeth.

"You would know, dad," Mannon said, grinning broadly.

"What I want, Father, is what I've always wanted. I helped preserve this little travesty and I want back in. At the top."

Apostos laughed. I moved from my chair to join Flesh.

"Heal me," I whispered, "If this goes badly, we need to move."

She nodded and slipped her hand over my form, subtly working her power. I felt then muscles begin to knit back into place.

"That will never happen," Apostos said, "You have served your purpose. You were a means to an end – not the end itself. You will never be what you were."

Mannon grabbed him by the throat.

"Says you," Mannon said.

Apostos struggled. Mannon stood up, his grip still firm. Apostos tried to wrestle free of his grip but could not.

"You tainted me with this, filled me with something you didn't even understand," Mannon growled, "Now feel its strength!"

Mannon reversed his grip and took Apostos' forearms in both hands. I could hear a subtle cracking and grinding of what must be bones underneath. Apostos began to rise.

"I will be back, Mannon, to destroy you utterly," Apostos shouted.

A bright flash of golden light exploded from his eyes. Mannon never flinched. What was that…one of our own?

The figure in Mannon's grip fell slack for a moment and then seemed to shake itself off. It cried out in pain and looked up at Mannon. A look of confusion came over Apostos' face and he looked around wildly.

"No! This is wrong! Who are you?"

Mannon's grin of triumph faded into a scowl.

"I should've known that he'd erase all trace of me, the bastard," he muttered, "That being said, it's nice to see you again, little brother."

"You're Mannon," Apostos said, his fear becoming delicious in the air.

"That's right, Apostos. But, enough about me…"

Apostos tried to pull away…Mannon opened his mouth wide and blackness yawned to swallow our adversary whole…

MICK

The nurse fell forward, dead, her neck bitten by one of the wolves…I screamed and blew his head off with Casey's gun, the recoil nearly throwing me from the rope. Nancy the nurse slid aside and the wolf went plummeting to the ground below. What the hell was this? This already happened. As I was struggling to get my grip on the rope and make my way down, Lichonus pushed himself up onto the window's ledge.

"You choose the shittiest things to dream about, you know," he said, "Let's go to that little café near the ocean in Trelaen."

And we were there.

I was sitting down on the chair, drinking the slightly-off coffee. I was about to toast the ocean again when Lichonus pulled up a chair next to me.

"Much better. Mick, I've been listening to everything that's been going on and I think you need to consider—"

"I'm not sure I should trust you, Lichonus. So far, you've cast some serious doubt on what I've been trying to do and haven't given me much to go on in return. Now, I have to worry about not only Father and the Kingdom, but a new player as well who calls himself Mannon. But, you already know all that."

"Your dreams are all I have to use right now, Mick. Do you want to hear me out or not?"

I took the last sip of the coffee and threw the cup over the seawall and into the ocean.

"I asked them to wake me up as soon as Apostos returned, or if he didn't come back in time. Be quick."

"Fine. I think the key to finding out what happened, to restore my memory, is to bring me to Mannon."

"What do you know about him?"

"Only what you do."

"Then how can you think that would be a good idea?"

"You're going to have to confront him eventually. Maybe even when you go to Trelaen."

What was Lichonus' angle here? I couldn't figure…whoops.

"My angle? You really are getting paranoid, Mick."

"With good reason. How am I supposed to trust anyone when I can't even trust by subconscious? It's tough figuring things out without having the counsel of my own thoughts."

"If we can find out what really happened, we can proceed with a clear picture. I figure maybe this Mannon can give me enough juice to restore what I've lost…he's chock-full of darkness, right?"

"So, it's been said. I don't like where this is going though. It sounds like you want us to cooperate with him."

"I just want to be put together again, Mick. I don't like the fact that I'm missing a good chunk of myself. Do you understand that?"

"Yes, believe me, I get you," I said, "I don't have all the answers either and it's hard to know what to do."

"Bring me to Mannon and maybe we can figure it out with what he may know. He can't be all bad, attacking the Kingdom like that."

"Yeah, I can't figure why he'd attack them if he's part of the darkness."

Lichonus frowned. I heard footsteps echoing along the street by the ocean. They were enormous.

"I think it's time for you to go," Lichonus said, "Think about what we talked about, Mick."

"How can I not?"

Someone gently shook my shoulder. It was time to go.

* * * * *

The sky burst forth with heavy, gray droplets from thick, overhanging clouds. We were assembled on the rise of the road leading into Trelaen. Lightning flashed through the gloom, illuminating the hell that seethed below us in the streets of the city. Legions of wolfmen and other twisted creations milled about, howling and gibbered in anticipation and bloodlust as we approached. On the other side of them, the great fortress stood, the place where Casey and I had spent some very miserable times. Its spires and minnarets pierced the clouds. From the windows of those towers, a garish red light spilled out. Hopefully, Apostos was still alive and whole inside, somewhere. The wolfmen we expected, but the other creatures were savage, dark creatures with blackened skin. Somehow, the wolves seemed preferrable to the others.

I strode forward, sword unsheathed and stood upon the precipice. On my right, Casey stood, her dark cloak trailing the wind, pistols gripped in her hands in readiness. Beside her, Otomo flickered in the lightning, his body shimmering like a ghost, his blade gleaming and hungry. On my left, Henri was smoking and held a gun-like weapon strapped over his shoulder, a mechanism festooned in gears, dials and gauges that I would never understand, but through his gifts, Henri had wrought. Dakum stood beside him, a giant, fearsome figure in bronze armour, his head covered in an open-faced helm that let the enemy see the grim determination on his face. His hands, the only weapons he needed, were formed into fists that were the size of my head. I raised my sword to the sky.

"Today, we destroy the Kingdom and win ourselves a home…I know I've given you all reason to doubt me and to question what we're doing here. The simple fact is that you realize, as I do, that we can't wander forever, broken-hearted and without roots. At least, I know I can't. We've all lost something or someone in the course of our awakening to this life and some of us have found something to care about again. It's all in jeopardy because of the Kingdom and because our creator will be forced to act if we fail. Let's prove to him and to all the worlds, that we deserve a home."

"Well said," Henri told me, adjusting the shoulder strap of his weapon.

"As we discussed, then," I said and strode down the road towards the open streets of the maw of hell.

The wolves bounded towards us in droves, their momentum carrying them far ahead of their twisted comrades. That was good. Henri opened up with the cannon. Green fire shot out in a solid stream, pouring out of the engine of Henri's genius. What the fire touched, it turned into a screaming mass of fur and claw that either collapsed on the ground to be trampled or was cut in half by my sword. Their eyes gleamed as they leapt at me. The first that got past Henri's gun lost his head. The next was shot twice by Casey. Another was crushed to the ground by Dakum. Still, others surged forward, crawling out from the avenues, and burning homes that were once part of beautiful Trelaen.

As we engaged the next group, I noticed that we were right by the baker's shop where I first came into the city. The windows were broken and the acrid smell of burning flesh drifted out of it, rather than the wonderful baked goods that I had so treasured. I ducked the blow of the first wolf that came at me and impaled him on my blade. That one was for the baker. I kicked him off my sword as three more passed through the gauntlet of our fire and bullets and made it into close quarters. I narrowly missed taking a slice across the chest and clove him down through his midsection. I realized my mistake as one of the blackened creatures appeared from behind the corpse, using it to get close. I pulled at my sword to get it free, but the monster was too close! It grabbed my fur-lined coat and began to pull me close to bite at me. I abandoned the sword for the moment and got my hands around its throat. I felt a round whiz by my head from Casey's direction…way too fucking close!

"I've got it, damn it! Don't blow my head off!"

At least, I hope I did. It was still lurching forward, trying to bite at me…bloody 'Falkir' one-oh-one! I reached up and put my thumb in one of its eyes. It quickly switched its tactic, screaming as I put my other thumb in. So gross. I didn't have time for this nonsense…we'd get surrounded if we couldn't clear these assholes in short order. I forced the creature to its knees and, with the leverage, broke its neck. My hands were covered in black goo. I wiped them on its corpse and retrieved the sword. I fell back a bit to join Casey. She blew away another wolfman.

"Have you got enough stored up?" I asked her.

"Almost," she replied.

In front of us, there was a wide thoroughfare cluttered with overturned wagons, burning piles of debris and the throng of Kingdom soldiers. Henri was firing sporadically over the street to keep the creatures back as we advanced; any that were brave enough to get past the fire were either gunned down or cut down. We moved slowly and steadily up the street. There were so many of the blackened creatures now…crowds of them in the buildings and more clamoring into the streets to stand in our way. The wolves were few in number by comparison. At last, we reached the boulevard that led up to the fortress. It was thick with the enemy. They were clustered around a fountain ahead and many more were swarming in from behind to surround us.

"Ready?" I shouted to Casey.

"As I'll ever be," she said.

"Okay…Otomo, Dakum, to me! Keep those things away from Casey. Henri – just burn the crap out of them!"

Henri lit a smoke from the chamber of his cannon and nodded. He looked very tired; I don't think any of us counted on how long we were going to have to use our powers for and the taxing onslaught of the Kingdom's forces. And we haven't even got into the castle yet…

Casey dropped to the ground, put away her guns and put her hands against the cobblestones. Under our feet, we could feel a vibration starting. The enemy seemed to sense that we were up to something and started moving in with a purpose. Otomo went ghostly and started moving, taking heads with an ease that was just unfair. I struck two down in a figure eight as they approached me. They were replaced by five more…

"Dakum! Little help here!"

I felt the air whoosh by me as he brought his hand across them, knocking them to the ground in a powerful sweep. They tried to get up, but I cut them down. It wasn't the fairest fight, but I was done with not using our powers to their fullest against those who don't fight fair either. The ground was really shaking now and I looked back to see that Casey's eyes were open, which was something she doesn't usually do when using this end of her power. Her eyes were brimming with energy.

"It's too much, Mick," Casey whispered, "Too much…"

"Let it go!"

Casey exhaled and then screamed long and loud.

Her scream was punctuated by a great groan below us. The creatures coming at us scattered as the cobblestones nearly exploded out from the earth and a great, green pine shot up and out from below. The roots shot out from the base, impaling several creatures. The branches covered half the street. I stumbled back from it as it spread out. At its crown, the tree was nearly forty feet tall and was at least fifteen feet wide. I picked up Casey from the street and held her.

"You know what's next," I said, turning to Dakum, "Let's get in there before it's too late."

Dakum reached out both of his arms, wide enough to encompass the tree and began to concentrate. His eyes glowed brightly and even the veins in his arms seemed to glow with an eerie light, under his skin. Henri looked at him with concern, then looked at me. I knew what he was thinking…probably promising me that if anything happened to Dakum, he would use all of his genius to find a way to make me pay. That's what I would think, anyway, if our positions were reversed.

"Cover us," I said to Henri.

The tree began to lift out of the ground, propelled by Dakum's insane strength and power. I helped Casey into the branches and clambered up after her. Otomo swiped his sword at me in salute and then began to march off towards the castle. The creatures died, cut down by his blade as they tried to get in his way.

We hung on to the tree as it floated over to the castle. I could now see a terrace, a couple floors up on it that would serve as some place to land. I looked back to Dakum and pointed frantically at the terrace. He nodded grimly, clearly running out of juice pretty quickly. I took Casey's hand and pointed out what I saw on the castle.

"Do you remember where that is from the inside?"

"No," she said, "But maybe it'll come to one of us once we get closer. Doesn't look like anybody's waiting for us, does it?"

"They're probably inside, with our luck," I said, "Are you okay? That was one hell of an effort back there…"

"It's a safe bet that I won't be doing that again anytime soon. My head feels like Dakum clapped his hands against my ears…next time, you make the giant distraction, okay?"

"I've never tried a tree, but there's always a first time."

We were now almost level with a terrace. The tree was beginning to sway…I looked back and saw that Dakum was on his knees, barely holding it together. There were a dozen or so creatures around both himself and Henri. Henri was burning them, but he was nearly done.

"Can you get down from here?"

Casey looked down as the tree began to sway more violently.

"If I time it right, why?"

"Dakum and Henri are toast if we don't do something…when I tried to plan this, I didn't count on so many of those creatures!"

We looked at each other and the tree started to fall.

"Go!" she screamed and she jumped down to catch a lower branch.

I wanted to look if she made it, but I didn't have time.

I jumped from the tree and grabbed hold of the terrace rail. The tree fell over, crashing to the ground and rolling around below. I heaved myself over the rail. The terrace doors were iron and they swayed in the wind as I watched them, my hand on my sword. After a moment, I crept up to the doorway and went inside.

FALKIR

We moved slowly up to the ship, where it hung in the air. The snows were deep here. This region was much like the place I was raised in Akilla, along the border with Sigda. There were snows there and mud in the snows and blood in the mud. I sometimes wished that I could live in that time again, as who I was now, rather than the sniveling child that the Akilla dragged through their campaign after taking my mother for their pleasure and making her pregnant with me. They could have just drowned me at birth, as I might have, but they did not. They had been weak. I had shown them all what true strength really was. Maybe that was what made me care for Flesh, some kind of weakness, some mercy that I hadn't yet burned from my soul.

She moved quietly a few paces behind me, dressed in a heavier robe and high boots. She had a sickle at her side, covered in soot from our fire before we set out. This needed to be done quietly. Behind her, a select group of the most controlled of her wolves crept through the snows and through the trees. As we approached the ship, I signaled Flesh to come around the other side and bring her wolves up with her. I made my way, as gingerly as I could, up one of the mooring lines and latched myself to the hull with my sharpest pair of knives. The ship swayed slightly and I heard footsteps on the deck above me.

"Come sit back down, Jack," I heard Penny say, "At least finish this hand."

"I wish Mick had taught the savage something besides poker," Jack said, irritated.

"You mad because you lose?" I heard another, unfamiliar voice, "You good at that, yeh?"

"A child's game," Jack muttered.

"You lose like child," the other voice said and laughed.

I heard a few hasty footsteps. A scuffing sound of a chair being shoved back quickly…Jack cried out in pain. Penny gasped.

"You're just a savage with no manners," she said.

That was my cue. I pulled myself up onto the railing and over.

There was a little lantern hung for warmth in a circle of chairs with a small, low table in the centre. Cards were scattered across the table and hot mugs of something spicy and sweet were sitting there steaming in the cold. Jack was standing, wiping something from the side of his face. Penny was sitting, wrapped up in a heavy blanket, her gaze locked on me as I crouched off in the darkness. Their captor, a giant, black-bearded man in furs, held an empty mug in his hand by one finger and looked very pleased with himself. A large, heavy axe was leaned against his chair, well within his reach. He seemed to notice the change in the air and tossed the mug in my direction. I took no notice of it and let him go for his axe.

"Falkir," Penny whispered.

Jack spun around towards me and pulled a small knife from a holster up one of the sleeves of his jacket. I smiled at him. What did he expect to do with such a tiny weapon? I chuckled, pulled out one of my larger daggers and tossed it to him.

"If it makes you feel better, Jack, take it with my blessing," I said.

He smiled, picked up the dagger and dropped into a low, balanced stance, one weapon pointed at my eye, the other at my gut. I liked Jack…he was a good killer of men.

"You might want to rethink your position, after taking in all of the facts," I said, nodding at Penny.

Penny was stock still, her eyes locked on the peripheral. Flesh was behind her two paces, her sickle in her hand. Jack spared a look and turned back to me. He dropped the dagger and the knife to the deck and moved to protect Penny. I nodded at Flesh and she let him join Penny.

"Are you here to kill us, then?" Jack asked, not taking his eyes from me.

"Mannon desires your presence," I said, "We are here to take you back home."

The bearded man stepped forward, axe in hand.

"I think not," he said.

The bearded man had a look of absolute disregard, looking back and forth from Flesh to me and smiling broadly.

"You are Falkir? Truly?"

"Yes and who are you who holds two of the Kingdom at bay?"

"Simmi," he said, "Some call be 'bear.' It is honour to meet you. Mick told me you were tough, good with a knife. He said you eat people. No worries, I no judge."

I was fascinated. This brute actually looked at me as an equal. I wondered if the arrogance would make his meat bitter, or merely sweeten my night with the relish of his death? I could hardly tell what kind of cut I would yield once I dug through the piles of furs…

"Mannon is a monster, Falkir," Penny said, trembling, "Worse than anything you could imagine…if you could only see—"

"I've seen what kind of monster he is," I said, "Believe me, I've seen more than you on that account, but I have little choice in the matter of who I follow now. Neither do you."

The wolves climbed onto the deck from their positions around the ship. They surrounded the circle of us on the deck.

"Enough talking," Simmi said, raising his axe and pointing it at me.

"You're right," I said, "But I promised our men that they would eat well tonight. In addition to my sins, I would not wish to add lies to the pile. You understand, of course, that the menu is very limited."

Simmi smiled at me and spun his axe in one hand. I whistled and the wolves began to tighten the circle.

MICK

The hallway was deserted too. I moved through with caution, scanning the walls and alcoves of the hall for places where Falkir or one of the wolves might be waiting to ambush me. I stayed out of the direct line of sight of the room ahead as well, not wanting to get burned by Nicholas' fire. I heard motion in the large dining hall ahead. There was the snarling and screaming of many voices and in the mix I could hear the perfect hum of a single blade. I had heard it before and each hum was punctuated by the absence of another snarling voice. Otomo was taking it to the enemy. As I reached the dining hall entrance, the sounds of combat suddenly ceased. I came around the corner, holding my sword up in a high stance to slaughter whatever fell beneath it.

Immediately at my feet were the dismembered and disemboweled corpses of several of the disgusting blackened monsters that we had encountered outside. One of them was still stumbling around, his arm missing, aimless and dying. Otomo sat in the middle of the room, cross-legged, his sword stuck in the wooden floor of the hall. His clothes were torn up, his face covered in the grime and gore of combat.

"Otomo! What—"

He raised his arm and pointed up above my head to a point behind me between two stained-glass windows. I nearly dropped my sword when I saw what he was pointing at.

"No…"

The thing that hung between the windows no longer resembled the person that I had once known. His face was mutilated, torn, and wrenched out of shape, his limbs the same, except they now ended in blackened claws. From each hand dangled a chain and on each chain was a skull impaled on a hook. One skull was dark-haired and in the hair were shells from a world I had never known. The other had a mocking look to it and a goatee that was distinctive and infamous. Lethia and Nicholas. The only clue to the identity of the body was a hooded tabard, shredded but still white in places where the blood and darkness had not blighted it.

"Get up, Otomo…get up and help me get him down," I said, my heart filling up with stones.

Otomo got up and we moved to take Apostos down from where our enemy had strung him up. I moved to take hold of one of his ruined arms. Otomo smacked my hand away.

"What?"

Otomo's brow was creased, as if trying to listen.

"Mick…"

Apostos one good eye opened. It was a milky white and it spun around frantically as if searching for something. His limbs twitched, his now-clawed hands flexing and dark blood oozed from the wounds in his chest. His breathing was ragged and raspy. He was now more human, in his suffering, than he had ever been. For some reason, it made me feel uneasy. Mannon had corrupted him, turned him into the same thing that Lichonus had been before Apostos himself had destroyed him.

"I'm here, Apostos," I said.

His eye stopped moving around and focused on me.

"I am sorry…he knows everything Mick…"

"What do you mean? What does he know?"

"All about us, about you…he knows what you carry…"

Oh no…

"Does he know where the others are?"

"I'm so sorry…" he said and stopped moving.

The blood stopped flowing. His eye closed. I heard footsteps. I spun around to see Henri being helped into the hall by Dakum. I breathed a sigh of relief as Casey walked in behind them, slightly limping.

They all stopped when they saw Otomo and me. Then, they saw the body.

"Who the hell is…"

Henri's eyes went wide and he went silent.

Casey ran up to me and I held her back as she tried to reach up to Apostos.

"Let me go, Mick! He was my friend too!"

I pushed her back.

"You can't, Casey," I said, "He's been corrupted."

She drew her gun.

"No. You know that I'm the only one who can end his suffering," I said, "The sword was made to destroy the darkness."

Casey backed off. Henri and Dakum joined us.

"The problem is that he told Mannon where we are and a lot of other things," I said, riffling my hair with my hands, "You guys have got to go back to the ship before he gets there…make sure Jack and Penny are safe."

"This was your plan, Mick! We. Failed. Now you're sending us off somewhere else?" Henri said, his voice strained and angry.

"It ain't his fault," Casey said, taking my hand, "How could he've known?"

"You sent Apostos here, Mick. You kept your secrets, followed all of this on faith and now Apostos is going to die, if he isn't already!"

My blood boiled. I knew some of what he was saying was the truth, but not all of it. For all we knew, Mannon was already heading to take out Jack and Penny. I reached up and pulled the chained heads from Apostos' hands.

"Lethia and Nicholas," I said, shaking the chains at Henri, "That leaves Falkir and Flesh, plus Mannon. See a trend, Henri? Get the fuck back to your ship!"

Casey looked at the heads spinning on the chains and grabbed Nicholas.

"That's one thing off my to-do list," Casey muttered.

She turned and fired her gun, opening up a portal to Tiroj. Henri glared at me and then staggered over to the portal with Dakum. Casey turned to Otomo.

"Coming?"

"What I said before holds true," he said, "The Kingdom is not destroyed and so I fight on."

Otomo pulled his sword from the floor and walked off to join the others.

"See you soon?" Casey asked me.

"One last thing to do here," I told her and I turned back to Apostos.

I heard her walk away behind me. The portal closed and I was alone with my dying companion. I drew my sword.

"I failed you and I'm sorry for not understanding, before, that you were just trying to protect the worlds…"

I heard a creaking above me and I looked up to see that Apostos' eye was opened and he was straining at the hooks and chains that held him to the wall. His eye held no life in it, though and was becoming blacker as he struggled. Black ichor began to drip from his open mouth. His face stretched into a gruesome grin.

"Hello, Mick…such a pleasure to finally meet you…"

I raised the sword to Apostos.

"Let him die, you bastard! Get out of him!"

"Oh, poor old Apostos isn't here anymore, Mick. He's gone over the rainbow. Moved on. It's just you and me, now…"

"So, you're Mannon?"

"After a fashion," he said, "Hell of a show you put on here…I watched through my many eyes as you and your friends hacked and crushed the pathetic creatures that once populated this city. Does it please you to know that you and yours have killed more people than I ever have?"

I considered his words…it was a mercy that those people died, wasn't it?

"What do you want, Mannon?"

"Well, that's the thing. This was merely to get your attention, more of a handshake really. I do have a couple of things you might want back though."

Damn it. He was way ahead of us now.

"Jack and Penny," I said.

He cackled, Apostos' jaw cracking slightly with the effort.

"Yes," he said, "Your friends went quietly. Except for the barbarian type you left to guard them…he was very stubborn."

"Is he alive?"

Mannon smiled.

"You rotten bastard!"

"Now, now, Mick…you shouldn't have left him to try and stop my new friends…as you know, they don't have much use for the weak."

I screamed and drove the sword into Apostos' chest. Mannon's face lit up with green fire and he howled with laughter as he burned. Before I could free the sword, he reached down, breaking free of the chains and grabbed my arms. I felt darkness surge into me. I fed all the energy I could muster to fight him as he tried to get inside me.

"I see that we're not alone after all," he croaked, as he burned, "I see you, old friend…"

Then, as I began to lose my grip, a white energy began to burn inside of Apostos. Mannon cried out and I poured on the juice. The white light began to enter me as well. I pulled the sword free. Apostos body arched and screamed in agony as it seemed to explode with green and white fires. In a moment, there was nothing left but ashes.

I fell down on my knees. My limbs seemed to jump and twitch with energy. Something was very wrong here. I fell forward, leaning on the sword. I had to get back to my friends…I had to help them…

"You can't even help yourself, Mick," Lichonus said, stepping forward from the shadows to my right, "What makes you think that you can help them?"

Lichonus was different now, clad in a stained, white robe over dark chainmail.

"What are you doing here? I thought you were restricted to visiting hours in my dreams…"

"He was," said a voice, off to my left, "But what else are brothers for except to elevate each other in their time of need?"

A shimmering white form blazed into my vision in the far-left corner. I shielded my eyes and the form dimmed as the figure stepped forward.

"Apostos…"

He appeared as he always had…white robes, chainmail, blond hair down his back and a lion wrought in silver upon a breastplate. What the hell was going on? Was I dead too?

"So, how do you feel about sharing your head with both of us?" Lichonus asked, reaching down to take my hand to help me up.

I took his hand. It was solid and he had a strong grip. I turned away from him and walked over to Apostos. He merely stood there, looking at me with his usual look of bemusement.

"You're in my head too? I should be charging you guys rent…"

"Well, after Mannon possessed me to taunt you, I decided to try and escape from my ruined form. As you know, I was with Father when we transferred all of you into the souls we sent out into the worlds and I helped him do so. I gambled that I could do the same with myself. Most of my essence, my energy, was released when you used the sword, but I smuggled enough to retain most of my personality."

Holy shit.

"Why the hell did you do that? It's crowded enough in here."

"Well, you owe me for one thing. That was stupid sending me blind into Mannon's clutches. Mind you, I doubt you realized what actually happened there, but nevertheless, that was a dumb move."

"Uh…"

"I also had enough time while Mannon was inside me to get a good look at his mind too. I learned a lot and I figured that you might want to know what is really going on."

I smiled to myself, thinking back to a time when he wouldn't tell me a damned thing. I felt a little relieved that maybe, just maybe, someone might be able to tell me what the situation truly is…I was tired of fighting in the dark, risking my friends and my life for a whisper and a promise.

"So, what is it that I don't know?"

"First things first…we must find the others; they will want to know as well. Mannon is a dangerous creature…"

A HISTORY LESSON

In the middle of a bright constellation of blue spheres, gigantic and ponderous in intent, sits a palace made of shining marble, a solid dome in the middle of it, ringed by a succession of towers made of the same luminous material. At the top of the dome, there is a crystalline cap that shines with an overwhelming green light. Inside that dome, seated at a large throne ringed by entrances from each tower, is an old man. His beard is long, his hair billowing and white and from his eyes burn the fiery light of all creation. He is Father and he is mighty.

At his side, he rests his hand upon a small iron lockbox decorated with glowing symbols that overlap each other and twist about, as if alive. With each drumming of Father's fingers, the symbols twitch. His patience is eternal, but his wrath often outreaches it. This day is typical in an eternity of days and he waits. Footsteps begin to echo from the entrance off to the left of the throne and Father turns to see his arrival.

A shepherd that appears as an older man with short dark hair and flat, grey eyes enters the chamber. He has a long, white tabard that is covered by golden plate armour with the image of a lion etched onto the breastplate. The chamber echoes slightly with his steps as his sandaled feet strike the floor. He stops directly before the throne and bows down.

"Rise, Mannon, my son," Father says.

Mannon rises and stands quietly before the throne.

"You are my favorite son, Mannon," Father says, smiling benevolently, "And it is to you I entrust a most precious gift to give to your people."

"I am honoured, Father."

"Take this box that I have here and bring it to your people. Open it for them and let them feast of its bounty. This is my will, Mannon."

"Your will be done, Father."

* * * * *

On one of those blue spheres, Mannon stands in the middle of a rolling sea of yellow grass that moves with the gentle breeze of a west wind. Around him, hundreds of men, and women, dusky-skinned and dressed in colourful clothes rendered from base textiles and dyed with pigments come to attend the one who has guided them and given them wisdom from on high. Mannon's heart fills with pride as he watches them come. In his hands, the symbols on the iron box given to him by Father literally writhe with energy, as if excited by an internal, eager will. He suspects nothing of what is to come.

"I have brought you all a gift from my father," Mannon says, "Gather close so that you may all share in it."

And so, they gather around him: fathers taking the hands of mothers, mothers taking the hands of their children, families heeding the words of their bright and holy benefactor. Mannon smiles at them and begins to undo the latch of the box. The symbols twitch for one last time and fly apart in fragments that fade in a wondrous golden twinkling. He opens the box wide. At first, there is nothing inside, only a dark, empty hole and his people look to each other, their wonder turning to apprehension.

Then, a whistling comes up from the hole and a giant gushing volume of black smoke shoots up into the air from the box. Mannon drops the box and stares up at horror at the dark thing that seems to hang in the air in a manner that seems predatory and terrible. He moves to get between them and the thing, but it is too fast…and too many!

The dark thing splits into several tendrils of blackness that swoop down swiftly to get a hold of as many victims as it can. Mannon is swept aside by the fury of their dark rushing and struggles to rise, watching as the tendrils begin entering the mouths, ears, and other orifices of his charges…they scream, fitfully and in terror, as the blackness fills them. All of those gathered collapse and fall to the earth.

Mannon weeps, watching the dark thing disappear. He moves to and from each person and finds that they live. He shakes them, trying to revive them. He lifts their eyelids and gasps…the darkness is within them, swirling in their eyes like dark worms. They stir. They begin moaning and growling. They look at each other with wild eyes and they do not seem to know each other. Mother shoves away child, husband turns on wife and brother turns against brother. In moments, the growling becomes screams of feral challenge! They begin to tear at each other. Mannon screams for them to stop.

One of the men leaps at Mannon and begins to beat his fists against the leonine breastplate. Mannon pushes him away, but he keeps coming. Soon, many of them start to throw themselves against Mannon, clawing, biting, tearing, and beating at him. It is too much for him and he reacts as he has never done before. His hands reach out to crush throats, break bones and pulverize flesh. He is an engine of violence, propelled by fear.

In moments, none of the people remained standing, many of them brought down by each other's mischief, but the rest consumed in Mannon's struggling to survive. He stands in the middle of them, again, his hands and tabard covered in blood and black ichor, his breastplate streaked with gore. Small rivulets of blackness drip down his chin and he feels a bitter taste in his mouth. He turns his face to the sky.

"What have you done!?" he screams, "What have you made me do?"

There is no answer. Mannon falls to his knees and he feels the darkness working through his very being. A whistling begins to rise within him as well. It carries a whisper and Mannon cocks his head to listen. Visions of blood, black fields full of burning fires and broken cities fill his mind. He begins to feel a new sensation begin to work its way through his core.

Mannon begins to laugh, his face contorted and wicked. He runs his bloody fingers down his face and his laughter becomes a long and monstrous howl.

* * * * *

Outside the blue spheres and beyond the bright and luminous palace, a man's shape appears. He is naked, bearing none of its previous adornment. His body is badly wounded and leaking black fluids into the emptiness of space. The veins beneath his skin begin to seize and pop in the vacuum. A long spiral of fluid spurts from his mouth and twists away. His fingers, once beautiful and pink, now blackened and clawed, reach out to the spheres, an act of hunger that cannot be sated. He seems to realize this as he feels death take hold of him and he curls up into a ball. His eyes are still open, frozen forever from the cold outside. He sees all he ever knew in these last moments. A life of duty, unbound. A brotherhood, broken. A secret locked away.

As all comprehension disappears from his eyes, a black sphere the size of the blue ones appears behind the drifting body. It gets larger as it moves closer to him…he sees it, the seconds of his existence ticking away to zero as the surface overwhelms him. He feels the cold being taken away from his body and the whispers that spoke to him before have come again. As the black sphere fades from view, its passenger begins to dream inside his broken shell…

MICK

I watched my friends as they made their way along the side of the warehouse where I resided along the lake. I could tell from his ponderous gait and lingering shadow that Dakum was walking ahead and Henri was creeping cautiously behind. I didn't see Otomo anywhere, but my vantage point on the catwalk, above the warehouse floor, didn't cover all the angles. I stayed in the shadows for a bit and nodded my head. I heard Casey start moving behind me. I turned around to watch her as she unlatched the gate for the freight elevator and stepped inside. She tipped her hat at me, smirked, and closed the gate. The elevator started moving down.

The space we occupied was a hasty setup that Casey had lived in long ago when she was on the run from the Kingdom before she met Apostos. A friend of hers from those days had set this up in perpetuity for her…she had saved his life when the Kingdom rolled through. It wasn't much, but we had the top floor of an abandoned factory, a set of six cots, a large industrial metal table and chairs, running water, electricity and, most importantly, a place to breathe, take stock and figure out what to do next.

We had parted company with Henri, Dakum and Otomo less than a week ago after I caught up to all of them in Tiroj. Tiroj…what a fool I had been to imagine that we had outsmarted Mannon…we were all being shuffled around the playing board and we didn't even know it until recently. Mannon had reached out with his minions and murdered my friends with ease. *Goddamn you, Simmi! Why couldn't you just run?* His death had unnerved me. I knew whose hand had rendered his finish and there would be a reckoning when I found Falkir.

Mannon had Jack and Penny as well. He left instructions for where they were and what we had to give him to get them back. The note was attached to Simmi's severed head, which had been driven through a long spike sticking up from the ground in front of the burning remnants of Henri's beautiful ship. I rubbed at my jaw as I remembered how he'd slugged me after he saw what they had done to his creation…Dakum pulled him off before things got serious. In truth, I doubt I would have stopped him from beating me within an inch of my life, because it's what I deserved for being so stupid. We were all running very close to the edge now and I had a feeling that we'd get even closer before it was all done. I went over to the steel table and sat down at the head.

…Penny for your thoughts?...Apostos muttered.

Are you trying to be funny?

…I do not know…I try to stay out of your mind and keep Lichonus occupied, but sometimes I hear stray thoughts and perceptions…

The thought of you developing a sense of humor is slightly hilarious in itself. I think you've been hanging around me too much.

…Possibly. I have little choice. Are the others here yet?…

Yeah, they're on their way up with Casey. Can you control Lichonus enough to get him to talk when everybody's here?

…I think so. The amount of dark energy he absorbed restored him to basically how he was from shortly before Father lobotomized him. He is very angry, but he will listen to me…

"That's good. I'd hate to have to shut him down; what he knows is critical."

"What who knows?" Henri said, stepping out of the lift, swiftly followed by Dakum and Casey.

"You'll find out soon enough, Henri," I said, rising to greet him.

"Why don't you and Dakum sit down over here and we can get started," I asked, gesturing at the table.

"That's fine," Henri said.

He stayed standing while the others sat down.

"Something on your mind?"

Henri pulled out a smoke and lit it. He crossed his arms and inhaled.

"First of all, I'm sorry I decked you."

"You had your reasons, Henri, I understand—"

He raised one finger. What now?

"But Dakum and I aren't at your damn beck and call. We came here to hear you out, but I don't plan on risking his life or mine unless we're all absolutely sure about it, okay?"

"Yeah, I get that," I said, "If you'll sit down and listen, I believe you'll find what I say of interest to you."

Henri nodded and sat down next to Dakum and Casey.

"Otomo?" I asked, moving to return to my seat.

Henri and Dakum exchanged a brief, but meaningful look.

"We haven't seen him since we parted ways at the wreck," Henri replied, tapping his ash off on a rough edge of table, "Are you that surprised that he's not here?"

"He did say that he was going to keep his word to me," I said, pondering his words.

"That could mean a lot of things, Mick," Casey said.

…He could be going to kill the rest of the Kingdom, Mick. He's powerful enough to give it a shot – that would fulfill his promise…

I thought about what Apostos said. Henri and Dakum could be hiding something and I was suddenly glad that the rest didn't hear that last one…maybe it was more on the nose than Henri or Dakum would admit. With or without Otomo, though, we had to get things started. I began building up power, drawing on both the light and dark energies in my body; this meeting would be taxing, but hopefully worth the effort.

"I'm sure we're all eager to get started," I ventured, "I guess Otomo will have to be caught up later."

"Fire away, Mick," Henri said.

I began by telling them about what happened after they left between me and Mannon while he occupied Apostos' body and all the things he said. I finished by telling them about how Apostos had saved himself. Henri was wide-eyed and even Dakum was in disbelief. Henri got up from the table and came really close to my face…uncomfortably close. He looked me over like a surgeon assessing a disease.

"He's really in there now too…" he said in a pondering tone.

"Yeah."

"How's your head?"

"I'm fine, Henri. Look, for this next part, I need you guys to bear with me. It may get a little…weird."

"Define weird," Henri said.

"Are you sure you're up to this?" Casey asked.

"We'll see."

I drained the wells of power that I'd been drawing together. Apostos had shown me a different way to use my power than I'd ever imagined…it was much more demanding, but extremely useful. I brought up the images of Apostos and Lichonus in my mind and began to give them form and shape with the power I'd gathered. I stretched out one hand towards a seat to my left and my other towards the right. I let the power slip out, gathering up the essences of my two passengers to give them form in our world. Within moments, Apostos and Lichonus sat at the table with us, although their forms were slightly translucent. Although it was a huge expenditure of power, I felt a certain amount of relief about having them out of my head for a time, however brief.

"How the hell did you do that?" Henri cried.

"Just takes practice, Henri and a certain amount of risk," I replied, massaging my temples.

"Who the hell is that?" Dakum asked.

Lichonus was in the strange armour that he had on after Apostos died. He looked much healthier than he had before, the weariness in his eyes and face gone and replaced by a driven countenance. Lichonus had his strength back and his mind…

"This is Lichonus," I said, "And he's here to help us."

Lichonus shifted his eyes at me and smiled. It wasn't a comforting look. I hoped Apostos was right about him.

Casey got up from the table and came over to put her hand on Apostos' shoulder. Her fingers rested there for a moment and she blinked. She never told me what happened to bring them together, but I knew it meant a lot to see him again, if only for a short time.

"Are you okay?" she asked him.

"I still exist, thanks to your man here," he said, taking her hand, "I cannot stay like this forever.

Eventually, I will have to go on to whatever state is reserved for my essence, but for now I am stuck with Mick."

"Any port in a storm," I said.

"Exactly," he replied.

Apostos joked, but I knew that he was scared. He was right that he couldn't stay inside me forever…in the long run, neither of us had any idea what would happen when his power ran out and I'd have to let him go. If 'heaven' was as miserable as he described, I hoped it wasn't his only option.

"It's great to have you back, Apostos, really," Henri said, "But we came here to get a notion of what comes next."

Apostos looked over at me and I nodded.

"Well, the good news is that Father is not going to be blowing up the worlds to get rid of Mannon anytime soon…"

"And the bad news?" Dakum ventured.

"Mannon is going to lay waste to the worlds and we are the only thing standing in his way."

"Or standing with him…" Lichonus muttered.

Henri looked over at him.

"What?"

Lichonus chuckled and turned away.

"Yes…that is going to be difficult to explain without the rest. So, listen."

Apostos related to us the story of what happened to Mannon and who he truly was. I had heard it before, but it didn't anger me less in the telling. I understood why Mannon was so angry. I also understood why Lichonus had done what he did -- I probably would've done the same thing, whether that was his influence on me, or by my own decision. That was his story to tell, though. All of this history was denied to us by Father's will to bury it. The conversation between us would be very different now.

"I'll tell the rest of it, if you don't mind," Lichonus said.

He got up from the table and began to pace.

"I found Mannon after Father had him unleash the darkness, which corrupted him in the process. We were good friends, back then. I can't describe to you how angry I was when he told me what Father had done…I decided then that I would never follow another order from our creator. I would have rather been destroyed then do so.

"Mannon gave me some of his power and we soon learned of where it came from…it was the Dark Sphere, a power that existed outside the gardens, outside the great experiment that Father had created, a living world that was as forceful in will and mind as Father was, but entirely composed of darkness and chaos. We fought to deny its influence, but our anger over being betrayed only fuelled its power over us. We gathered a few of the other shepherds, sharing the yoke of his power with them and rebelled against Father.

"Those who we didn't recruit, who came to his defense, we struck down. We weren't howling beasts, as Father tried to depict us as in his tampered memories, but warriors bearing the sigil of the Dark Sphere, the memory of which he desperately tried to bury. In the end, only Father's honour guard remained loyal to him…Apostos, Sibelius, Pentalus and Naxos. Father chose to convey his wrath through them, literally and destroyed our physical shells. That much is true. He exiled Mannon from the worlds, sealing off the world that had been his charge."

"He decided not to waste what was left and sealed the essences of all who had been corrupted in the souls of emerging human beings," Apostos continued, "Still trying, apparently, to force the creation of a divine being through combining both energies. He fed me this truth to get me to help him and erased all of my knowledge of it after. He thought he did, anyway."

"We're all corrupted, then, aren't we?" Henri asked.

"Yes," I said, "And Father would have had me put my blade in all of you to destroy it."

I took Casey's hand and continued.

"I knew that I would never have seen that world that he promised; there's too much corruption in me to allow me to ever set foot on it. I didn't know how to tell you all that, but there it is. As it turns out, I think Father would have tried to force me to destroy all of you as well. That was before Mannon's return, of course."

"And now?" Dakum asked.

"Now, we do something of our own choice, of our own will and give Father a reason to keep his promise. We gather up the darkness, stick it back where it belongs and we kill Mannon and his fucking monsters."

FALKIR

We walked together in silence down the long corridor of the old tunnel beneath the temple that led to the cells where Lethia's people used to keep the sacrifices for their gods. The walls were smooth granite, polished by dutiful servants that were long dead, their craftsmanship lost to time. Not that Mannon would have cared, had I the mind to mention it…Lethia had shared her knowledge of this place with all of us when we were scouring the worlds looking for…well…whatever it was. This civilization had died when she was reborn, consumed when she was sacrificed on an altar, when she rose again to take her vengeance. Legends would have been passed on to future generations if she hadn't been so bloody greedy for death; she and Mannon would have gotten along well if he would have tolerated her existence. I had a feeling that, just like Lethia, no one would be left alive to speak of Mannon's atrocities.

Mannon had given up the suit that he had worn when we had first encountered him and now wore leather trousers and a ring vest. On his bare chest, there was a broad tattoo of a black sun whose rays bent and distorted to become tendrils that wrapped around his arms, neck, shoulders, and hands. They ended at his fingertips and his face. He seemed taller, now. It was as if he was growing, becoming a clearer expression of something we had only seen a piece of. As dark as my soul had become, I still felt dwarfed by the depth of what was inside him.

The torches in the tunnel flickered as we passed by, the cool air pushing along as we made our way down. I spied Flesh standing guard by the cells as we drew closer. She had become much more martial since Mannon had used her to create more monsters; she was less a den mother now, than a female alpha wolf. She no longer hid herself beneath a cloak but dressed in a dark red body-glove with high boots and a pair of sickles fastened at her hips. We hadn't talked much since she had changed…I had suffered from her absence…I did not like it.

She looked up at us as we descended a small flight of stairs into the room that housed the cells. It was circular, with all the cells on the outer perimeter. Light came from a round tunnel that entered the room from the ceiling. Daylight shone down, nearly sixty feet above our heads. It disappeared as the tunnel continued past the floor of the room and went deep. Flesh nodded at us as we approached. Her eyes shifted as one of the prisoners leapt at the bars of his cell.

"Let us out of this hole, you sons of whores!" Jack shouted, his hands hauling at the bars.

If it were any other day, I might kill him for that.

"Not very fond of prisons, Jack?" Mannon asked, moving up to the bars.

"Not so much," Jack said, "What do you want from me, Mannon? Whatever the price for our freedom, I'll gladly pay."

"You? I want nothing from you, Jack. I'm not here for you," he said, smiling at Jack.

Jack threw himself against the bars, reaching out for Mannon.

"No! Leave her alone!" he cried.

"Falkir! Please, don't let him hurt her," he continued, "You can't truly believe this madman!"

"I—"

Mannon turned to me and slapped a heavy hand on my shoulder.

"Oh, I think our relationship has been firmly established," he said, "We know where each other stands, don't we, Falkir?"

I despised the monster. As much as Jack's words moved me to rise up and put my blade in Mannon, I knew I couldn't do bugger all against him; I had tried before and been handed my own ass back to me on a platter. I merely nodded in agreement and said nothing more. All the while, I delighted in visions of throwing Mannon's corpse down the hole, minus his eyes and his balls.

Mannon shrugged his shoulders at Jack and moved in a delighted little dance towards the next cell.

"If you were ever my ally, Falkir, I beg you," Jack whispered, "Don't let him touch her."

I moved past him and stood by Mannon as he approached the cell where Penny was kept.

Penny was shivering in the corner of her cell, suffering from the dampness that crept through the stone to steal your warmth and set your teeth chattering. She immediately focused on Mannon and did not look away. Mannon motioned for Flesh to open the cell and grabbed up a torch from the wall. Flesh opened the door.

"Pretty Penny," Mannon said as he entered, "Gatherer of whispers, star-crossed lover, and black-hearted murderess. Bet you never told Jack that last part, did you?"

"All you know is the darkness inside us, Mannon," she whispered, hoarsely, "You know nothing of what makes us human."

"In my opinion, an opinion I've well-earned long before you and the others were crudely fashioned by Father's failing hand, your humanity is merely a shadow of the darkness that I know and love so well."

Mannon knelt down beside Penny and took one of her hands in his. She cried out and tried to pull away from him, but he laughed and pulled her closer. Jack yelled out from his cell and I heard him thrashing inside. Flesh's eyes found mine. There was very little concern there, merely a feigning look of disinterest. Was she lost to Mannon's darkness?

"The power that I cling to has never lied to me, has never betrayed me, and has shown me the true heart of the human condition. I serve it so that my former master, the architect of folly, may be shown the error of his ways."

"What has any of this to do with me?" Penny asked.

"Pieces on a game board," he said, "But fear not, for your own importance is at hand. Whether you know it or not, Penny, you're going to help me make it all happen. I have to make a call…"

"I'd rather die," she said.

Mannon reached up and grabbed her by the back of her neck. He pulled her closer to him.

"You *will* serve your purpose, Penny," he whispered, "Even if it kills you."

I couldn't take any more of this. I reached out to grab his arm. Flesh grabbed me before I could touch him and pulled me away. I looked into her eyes. There was nothing in them for me. She *was* lost.

"Get him out of here!" Mannon roared, "You're lucky I don't lock you up with them, dog!"

Flesh guided me up the stairs. As we moved along the tunnel, I could hear Penny's helpless screams mixed with Jack's frantic protests. Then, a deep, sonorous voice filled the tunnel and all was quiet.

"Hearken unto me," it said.

MICK

"We *think* it will work."

There was a stunned silence in the room. Casey and I were packing up some things after Henri and Dakum went downstairs to talk over what I had told them. Casey had asked me, point blank, how I intend to defeat Mannon and I told her. I wasn't surprised at her reaction. Even I had my doubts.

"What do you mean, 'you think it will work'?"

"Apostos says that, based on how he's able to draw the essence out of one being and put it in another, that it should be kind of the same for the darkness…it makes sense…"

"Holy hell, Mick," she said, "And how exactly are you going to store this darkness?"

"That's the part that you're not going to like," I said, looking at my boots.

Casey considered it for a moment and the grabbed me by the collar of my shirt.

"Inside you?"

I nodded. She pushed me back and shook her head.

"That's just plain stupid," she said, exasperated, "What's to stop all that darkness from corrupting you?"

"I'm hoping that the sword will be enough to fight against its influence; it's worked so far."

"This is a bad idea," she said, "Why are you so eager to throw your life away? What about me?"

This was one of the things I just couldn't handle right now. I'd tried to keep things easy between us, but I loved Casey and it was hard to make these decisions without her. All the same, I felt I had to. After all, I contained the essences of both light and dark and I intended to use them both to free us all. How could I even think about myself when the worlds were going to end?

"If I can get rid of the darkness and defeat Mannon, then I'll have a bargaining chip to use with Father. Don't you see that I'm trying to save us all?"

"At the cost of your own life! Every time, Mick – every time it's you on the hook for it! Aren't you tired of playing the fool?"

"I'm no fool!" I shouted back at her.

Casey blinked, grabbed her pack off of her cot and went over to the freight elevator.

"Where are you going?" I asked.

She pulled the gate over and stepped inside.

"Casey?"

"Somewhere to think!" she said.

The gate closed. The elevator headed down to the main floor.

I shouldn't have got so mad. I couldn't tell her how dangerous what I was going to do really was…absorbing the darkness from all my friends and storing it inside me…cancer in a box. The pressure was on and Mannon was ahead of us on this road to Armageddon. Either the pressure was getting to me, or I was changing because I was overloaded inside; whatever it was, I had to get a hold of myself. If I lost Casey, this would all be for nothing. What's the point in saving the world when the world was only worth saving because of who lives in it? It was selfish to think that way, but it's the truth.

A few moments later, the elevator started up again, headed up.

I stood in front of the elevator to greet her…maybe she'd cooled off. It opened. Henri stomped out and poked me in the chest.

"Are you out of your mind?" he growled.

"She told you," I said.

"Oh, she told me," Henri continued, "Between cursing your crazy ass, I clearly remember something about taking the darkness out of us and putting it into you!"

"It will work, Henri. You're an inventor, right?"

"A damned good one," Henri said, cooling down a bit and pulling out a smoke.

"Think of it as an energy transfer from one storage container to another…the mechanism, Apostos, regulates the flow and makes sure that the connection isn't interrupted while it's being transferred."

"Don't patronize me, Mick. Speaking my language doesn't make it sound any less dangerous."

"Really? It took me a while to come up with that…"

"Good for you! Mannon used the darkness to rot Apostos to the core. How do you expect to not have that happen this time?"

"He won't have to hold onto it forever. Just long enough to give me time to find Mannon and use it to stop him."

"We don't even know where he is."

"We'll find him."

"Hmm," Henri said, looking over my shoulder, out the window.

I turned around and looked outside.

The warehouse we lived in overlooked the waterfront on one side and a large parking lot on the other for the attractions at the pier. It was empty this time of night. The streetlights were turning off, one by one, as we watched. It wasn't dawn yet.

I ran over to the window. The lights weren't turning off…they were shattering!

"Did you feel that?" Henri muttered.

"Feel wha—"

Some of the gear on the table started rattling. I could feel the vibration under my feet. An earthquake?

"Get down!" Henri screamed and tackled me to the floor.

The windows blew inward in a shower of glass. The force that hit them drove the shards into the walls. I would've been reduced to chunks if Henri hadn't grabbed me.

"What the hell is going on? Where are the others?" I whispered.

"Downstairs, last I saw," Henri replied.

I was about to rise when a small tremor shook the building slightly. Then, another. And another. I crept up to the window ledge, dragging Henri over with me.

"On three," I said, quietly.

Henri nodded.

"One…two…three," I counted out.

Henri and I stuck our heads up to look out. We saw what was causing the tremors. We retreated.

"I think we're in a lot of trouble," Henri said.

"Oh my, yes."

The towering figure in the parking lot was nearly ten feet tall. It was a giant, dressed in golden armour that was very familiar, with a lion emblem etched on the breastplate. He had long, red hair and a great beard that spilled over his chest like molten lava. He bore a very large, ornate axe in each hand and he was looking around out there with glowing golden eyes, grinning broadly.

…Um…

What?

…Perhaps this was not a great time to move in…

Who is that?

…Our brother Naxos. He is Father's enforcer…

I thought that's what you did.

…I died. He does not waste much time…

So, he's your replacement?

…Apparently…

He looks pretty nasty. He looks tougher than you…how's that work?

…I am supposed to be subtle. He mostly destroys the subject of Father's wrath, whereas I just send them away. He especially enjoys crushing those who have a certain trait more than any other…

What would that be?

…Disobedience… Lichonus said, chiming in.

The blade of a giant axe-head crashed through the wall five feet behind us and we went flat to the floor as half the building started to give way.

FALKIR

I hated being in chains more than anything and Mannon knew it. I lifted my arm and felt the weight of the shackles. They were strong…there was no portal that would get me away from this. I was beginning to think that I'd chosen the wrong side.

They had me chained to one of the supporting pillars of the temple, near enough to the base so I couldn't rise up fully to my feet. I wanted to get away from this place now that I had heard the voice of something unspeakably powerful coming up from the chamber where Penny and Mannon had spoken together. My jailer and former lover, Flesh, had been the one to lock me up; she was lost to me now, perhaps forever, unless I could find a way to free her from Mannon's power.

From where I was chained up, I could see the grand stairway that led up from the dungeons below and the outer perimeter of the ruins around the pillars that made up the majority of the temple grounds. The air was very still and was heavy with moisture. It would rain soon, probably becoming a deluge. All I had were my clothes and my boots…they had taken everything else. Everything they could see, anyway. The wolf lurked underneath my skin, tempting me to lash out and become strong enough to break the chains. Mannon would kill me in short order if I tried.

Speak of the devil…

Mannon strode up from the stairway and began to walk towards the city ruins. Flesh followed, pulling a chain up from below that I couldn't see the end of. Jack stumbled up into the light, his face bruised and his hands shackled to the chain in Flesh's grip. She yanked him along as she followed Mannon. Jack was the only one that seemed to notice me. He looked confused by my circumstance but made no other action as Flesh pulled him forward. I moved as close as I could from my shackles to see what was going on.

Mannon stopped. Flesh pulled Jack up to her and pushed him to his knees.

"Bring them to me, Jack, as we discussed," Mannon said, "After all, you want to see Penny again, don't you?"

"I don't know what you've done to her," Jack said, "But I will make you suffer if she's any less the person I knew…"

He said the last, turning his gaze to Flesh, who said nothing in return. If Penny had been the focus of Mannon's power like Flesh had been, then Jack was in for a shock when Mannon reunited them. I hated Mannon for his lies and his manipulations…his use of my father's image in my dreams when we first met seemed more and more appropriate; my father had known all of the strings to pull to make me dance when I was weak. For that reason alone, I had resolved to find a way to kill Mannon. All of us had desired power and the death of our enemies, but not like this. Mannon was dangerous in a way that defied the boundaries of our conflict. I knew what I would do if I got free of his control.

"I'll do what you ask," Jack said.

Jack's eyes glowed. What was he looking for? I thought this world was deserted…

Several dozen people in business suits and casual clothes stumbled forward from the outer ruins, their faces drenched in sweat but otherwise blank. I saw that their eyes were glowing. Jack had them…but where the hell did they come from? I got my answer as a small team of wolfmen moved in after them and surrounded the group. Flesh brought imports. Mannon looked them over.

"Yeah…they'll do," Mannon said, "I believe that, where they come from, they would be called 'takeout.' Lash them to the pillars, Flesh, as we discussed."

Mannon turned from the crowd and walked over to me.

"Come to gloat over whatever mad scheme you've hatched?" I asked.

"No but thank you for the compliment. I just thought I'd let you know that you're going to have company. Not for too long, mind you, but, for the time being, enjoy."

I was about to reply when Flesh pushed a man into view and bound him to the pillar next to me. He was dressed in overalls and had a slight beard and sunglasses. A cap was pulled down over his head. He said nothing as Flesh chained him up.

Mannon noticed my rapt attention towards the man.

"Hungry, are we?" he asked..

"As a matter of fact, yes," I said.

I was hungry, but the situation had just changed considerably. For the first time, Flesh nodded at me from behind Mannon and pressed one finger to her lips. I struggled at my chains.

"Come on! Just one? I'll be quick and I'm much better behaved when I'm fed."

"I'm afraid not. I have a use for these people that transcends your petty love of the long pig, Falkir."

"There's no accounting for some people's taste."

Mannon chuckled and turned away from me to address the others.

"Hold these people here and keep an eye on Jack while I bring Penny up for the festivities. They are not to be harmed. See Jack? I keep my promises."

"Just as long as you know that I will too," Jack replied.

Mannon laughed and went down the stairway to the dungeons. I looked over to the man chained beside me on the other pillar. He looked over to me, his dark eyes peeking out from over his sunglasses. Flesh came over to us, bringing Jack with her.

"How long do we have?" the man asked.

"Ten minutes, perhaps?" Flesh said.

Jack did a double-take and almost lost control of the people that Mannon had kidnapped.

"Oh shit…you!"

The man became silvery, translucent and the chains fell to the earth as he did a quick flip to his feet. Otomo took off the cap and sunglasses and tossed them aside. In a split second, Flesh's sickles were in her hands. I was about to tell her to stop, but she whirled around, away from us and killed the wolfmen, her children, in quick succession.

"You should have waited, Otomo," she said, "I didn't want to do that."

Otomo shrugged.

"If we're getting out of here, we better go now," he said.

"I'm not going anywhere with you and I'm not leaving without Penny," Jack said.

"Then stay," Otomo replied, "You will be very missed."

Flesh unlocked my chains. I smiled at her, rubbing my wrists. She smiled back at me.

"We're all going together," she said.

I stood up and hauled Jack to his feet.

"It's either we all go now, or none of us get out of here alive…you know he's going to destroy us, sooner or later," I said.

Jack's face twisted…he was on the verge of tears..sickening!

"I can't leave her," he said.

Suddenly, there was screaming all around the circle as Jack accidentally released his control over the hostages…a number of them began to scream and whimper as they realized that they'd been taken. Our window to get out of here just got shortened. There was a distant howling below in the tunnel and we all turned to the stairway.

Otomo began to make sigils in the air, opening a portal.

"We need to go," he said.

A roaring that sounded like the rush of water sounded from the tunnel. A second later, a black cloud of darkness exploded from below and began to grow solid.

Mannon stepped out from the cloud, wisps clinging to him as his form became solid.

"No one is leaving," he said.

Flesh put her hand out, on my chest, over my heart, smiled and tossed me Jack's chain. Our eyes locked and I knew what she was going to do.

I pulled Jack with me, fighting my instinct to stay with the woman I loved. Bigger things, her eyes had said. She leapt at Mannon, her sickles still wet with the blood of her children and began to cut at him. He laughed as the blades dug into him and he grabbed at her. I watched as they went tumbling down into the tunnel.

"No! We can't leave!" Jack sobbed.

"You don't have the market cornered on suffering, asshole," I said, moving towards the portal.

The world inside the portal was all night and city lights. From somewhere close, inside, I heard a huge rumbling. There was some kind of explosion.

"This doesn't seem like much of an escape," I said to Otomo.

"Come on!" he shouted, moving into the portal.

I pulled Jack with me, wondering if I'd ever see Flesh again. Jack resisted me, but we went through. A cold wind blew on that side…

MICK

"I know you are there, Apostos…bring Mick to me and all will be forgiven!"

Naxos' voice was deep and resounding and tinged with a definite undertone of impatience. I had no doubt that if anyone in a few miles' radius had also been called 'Apostos,' they might have just shat themselves. I was close. Henri, his hair whiter than usual with plaster dust, puffed at one of his locks that hung in front of him.

"I think it's for you," he said.

Half of the top floor had crumbled from the front onward. We were lying on the other side of where Naxos' axe had impacted. There was a good chance that the place was not long for this world. We had to get out of here and find the others, make sure they're okay.

…Them, yes, but not us…

Say again Apostos?

…Naxos has found me because he can sense my presence, Mick. The others will get away without issue, but us…not so much…

"That's great," I muttered.

"What's great?" Henri asked.

"Apostos is saying that the very bad man with the axes outside is Father's beating stick and guess who he's homed in on."

Henri pulled his pistol from his coat and pounded his chest lightly.

"Word is bond," he jeered, "Let's get him."

Another huge strike hit the building and a little more of our hiding spot crumbled away. I heard a groaning and I watched as the ceiling started to give way in the area beside us. We either made a break for it now or would be taking the express route to the main floor very shortly along with the top floor.

"Portal out, back to your world," I said, "I'm going to crawl down the elevator shaft and get the others to do the same."

"What about you?"

"I'll follow when it's safe."

"It's never been safe yet."

"Okay. Less dangerous, then."

"Deal. Make sure Dakum's safe, or I'll electrocute your testicles," he said, grinning.

Henri drew a design of a door in the air and disappeared into it.

I crawled quickly over to the elevator and nudged the gate open. I slipped inside and pulled out my sword. I got to my feet and drove the sword downward, cutting into the floor to make room for myself. I kicked out the rest of the boards and paneling and dropped down, grabbing hold of the remaining floor.

The elevator shaft had a maintenance ladder built into the side. I spied it off to my right and swung until I got enough momentum to basically throw myself at the ladder. I scrambled and managed to get one hand and one foot into the rungs. I was lucky that jumping off boats and running for your life from people who wanted to kill you keeps you in shape. I took a breath and began to climb downwards.

A voice spoke from somewhere below me.

"I'd know that ass anywhere."

I looked down and saw Casey climbing up the shaft, Dakum behind her holding a small flashlight in his teeth and looking unhappy.

"You two have got to get out of here," I said, "I already sent Henri back to Bersingholt – you need to follow him!"

"Why? What's going on?" Casey asked.

Large, thudding footsteps echoed from down on the main level and they were getting closer.

"The hand of god has come to punish me," I said, "And he'll keep coming until I figure out how to get rid of him. Now, could you please portal out before I get all of you killed?"

Dakum reached his hand out and began to shape a portal on the far wall. Casey looked up at me from down below.

"This is a lousy way to get out of an argument."

"Take care of everyone until I get there, love," I said, "I'll be fine."

"You believe that?"

"My mother raised me on fairy tales, so sure, I believe it."

"I love you, Mick."

"I know. Get going before the psychotic shepherd from hell downstairs cuts us in half."

"Had she lived, I'm pretty sure my mom should've warned me about guys like you."

"Most likely."

She smiled and leapt with Dakum into the portal on the far wall. Mission accomplished.

The axes punched right through the wall below me, shattering the ladder and shaking the whole shaft. I heard the elevator car above me start to groan. There was a huge tear in the shaft now and it was about to get bigger. I had no place to go but down. I let go of the ladder and dropped downward.

I caught hold of the ledge of the tear and started to pull myself up. A huge hand grabbed me by one arm and pulled me up and out of the shaft, tearing my coat and scraping me along the jagged edge. I felt a trickle of blood roll down my side and I had a terrible, dizzying moment of falling uncontrollably before Naxos caught me and held me up before him. His golden eyes scrutinized me with a predatory gleam, assessing and devouring.

"You do not look like Apostos," he said, "So you must be Mick. Strange…I can sense him here, yet he is not…what have you done with him?"

"He's dead. His shell was destroyed by Mannon."

"Truly? I do not know that name. Of whom do you speak?"

Of course, he didn't know…why would Father tell this brute anything?

"It doesn't matter. Apostos is inside my head now, sharing my shell, as it were. Could you let me down?"

Naxos grunted and dropped me to the concrete floor. I landed on my shoulder and rolled over, holding my scratched-up side. I reached inside my coat and felt the weight of the gun that Casey had picked out for me. It would not be my preferred way to get out of this, but it might be a good distraction.

Can this guy be killed?

…The sword can probably hurt him, but not kill him. The armour is the problem…the darkness can punch through it, but it would take a while…

"Father has sent me here to remind you to get to your task and keep your nose out of any heretical nonsense you may encounter on the way," Naxos said.

"And if I refuse to go through with our deal? I mean, he is a liar and a cheat."

Naxos took a swing at me, but I was ready and ducked aside with ease. He was probably too used to low-hanging fruit that went down without a fight.

"Father does not lie…he does not cheat!"

"He did and he does, Naxos."

"Since you know my name, then you also know that such arguments are pointless."

"Just shut up and obey?"

"Yes or be punished."

I pointed at him.

"Then you can tell Father this: No."

"Is that all you have to say before I crush your heretical soul?"

"Well, there is one more thing."

I swapped the gun in my jacket into my hand. It was semi-automatic, with ten rounds in the clip. I fired every one of them into his face. He fell backward, grabbing at his wounded head.

Thank you, Casey.

I bolted for the warehouse doors and cleared them just as Naxos began screaming for my blood. The bullets would just piss him off…I needed to tip this fight in my favour, somehow.

This neighborhood was quiet, save for our little conflict. Most of the people operating in this area were either criminals or derelicts. There would be no help to distract Naxos around here from the people. I had no idea how to operate most of the factory equipment in the places around me…wish Henri was here! Damn!

Heavy footsteps thudded across the street behind me. How could I get away from something that could track me by something I couldn't remove?

…Maybe we can distract him…

Conserve your power. I'll figure something out.

I ran into an alley, hopefully narrow enough to slow down Naxos if he tried to move in. Then again, he might just chop his way in with those axes. I was about to start down the alley when a man dropped down, barring my way. I tried to push him out of the way, but he wouldn't budge. He held up his hand.

"Hold, Mick," Otomo said.

It was Otomo…he was dressed in overalls and had no weapons that I could see.

"You're late."

"I was detained," he said, "But I brought reinforcements…it seems you may need some."

He pointed upwards, drawing my gaze.

I pulled my sword and dodged backwards. Falkir and Jack were standing on the fire escape above us. Jack lazily swung a chain in one hand and Falkir looked down at me with a reserved sense of malevolence. They made no move to attack me.

"You keep some interesting company, Otomo."

MICK

I lowered my sword and put my back up against the wall. Otomo made no move to attack me either, so that was a relief. Jack was looking worse than when I saw him before, thinner, and more ragged than his usual well-kept self, no doubt due to his incarceration by Mannon. Where was Penny? Falkir…well, he was bloody Falkir. I gazed up at him.

"You and I have business, Falkir," I said.

"Yes, we do," he replied.

I sighed.

"But not right now. I take it you're here to help in some way, Otomo?"

"What's happening?" he asked.

Falkir was the first one to perk up as Naxos approached. He leapt over to the top of the next building. Jack frowned and climbed up higher on the stairs to get a better look.

"He's a big one," Falkir mused.

"He's Father's enforcer," I said, "And he's here to punish me for defying him."

"Normally, I'd let him beat you to a pulp, Mick," Falkir said as Naxos drew closer, "But I think we might need each other before all is said and done."

"That's all that's stopping me from putting my sword through your chest again, asshole."

"We shall see."

Falkir cleared the building in one leap and struck a hard kick against Naxos' head. Falkir landed on his feet a few paces away and ducked the axe that Naxos swung to decapitate him. Otomo went transparent and moved out from the alley. Jack's eyes lit up with power. I had no idea what he was doing, but I hoped it was good. I gripped my sword in both hands and came out to face Naxos.

His face was a mess…the bullets hadn't drawn blood, but had blown the tissue all to hell, leaving a gleaming skull underneath, shot full of holes. A single, gleaming golden eye looked out from that mess and it settled on me. He swung his axe downward to chop me in half.

I went down on my knees, the sword barely holding back the ferocity of the blow. Otomo moved in, making his legs solid enough to kick Naxos' knee out from him, sending him staggering backward a step. I got up and moved forward, sending a cut across his chest. The armour deflected it, but the sword left a distinctive scar. Naxos bellowed in rage and swung the axe in a wild arc that took out the wall behind us in a shower of broken shards of brick.

I heard a ferocious howl and Falkir jumped on to his back, his wolf form complete with huge jaws and claws. He held on to Naxos other axe, strapped across his back and began to dig in and bite at him. Naxos struck with his free hand, landing a couple hits that pushed Falkir back, but didn't dislodge him. I struck at his breastplate, but only dented it. Otomo tried, once again, to kick out Naxos' legs, but he was too strong to take down that way. We both backed off as the axe went flinging around again.

"So hungry!" Falkir growled, digging at Naxos.

Naxos slipped his grip upward on his axe and used it to poke at Falkir. The small, bladed end cut along Falkir's chest. Falkir grabbed the axe and locked his other arm around the neck of the giant.

An engine roared in the distance and we were all bathed in the light of several pairs of headlights from down the street. They were getting closer.

"Jump, Falkir!" Otomo yelled.

Falkir turned to see the cars coming and leapt off Naxos.

The first car to run Naxos over was a little grey sedan. It hit him and he staggered backward, burying his axe in the hood. He had no chance to move before a larger, older red pickup truck plowed into him, throwing him back against the wall of the warehouse.

A large recreational vehicle was the last. It slowed down when it passed us. I saw the driver give us a green-eyed wink as it accelerated towards the warehouse. Naxos was bowled over, beneath the vehicle. It drove him back as well and into the ruined warehouse. I knew what was coming next.

The warehouse collapsed on top of Naxos, the iron-wrought supports staying vertical, but all the lesser materials falling down to bury him. Tons of wood, plaster and machinery crushed the vehicle as well. A few seconds later, a small explosion erupted from inside as it went up. I was about to move in when a hand gripped my shoulder.

Jack stood behind me, his eyes still glowing.

"I'm not done yet, Mick."

I heard a great groaning of metal from above us.

A huge, industrial crane was slowly moving across us from above, swinging a huge girder from some nearby construction project. Jack held up a hand to his ear as the crane's long arc moved over the warehouse.

"Wait!" I cried.

It dropped the girder.

The huge piece of metal came down on the warehouse with the force of utter devastation. The impact nearly threw us off our feet and I heard car alarms start going off all around the area. A thick plume of dust rose in the air and my ears rang with the sound of the girder's impact. Jack's eyes returned to normal and he dusted off his hands.

"Are you done now?" I asked.

"Yes. Just needed to work out some rage, Mick."

I started running towards the other vehicles, containing the people that Jack had taken possession of.

"Don't we all, you bastard," I grumbled.

MICK

Someone groaned from within the grey sedan that first ran over Naxos. In all the confusion, I forgot that Jack was using people to carry out his attacks against Father's thug. A delicate, white hand reached out from the driver's side and fiddled with the handle of the door. It pulled and pulled at the handle, but the door wouldn't open. The red truck that had hit him was untouched. A fellow in a plaid shirt, an old cap and jeans got out and ran towards us. He took one look at us as he got closer and turned back to help whomever was in the other car.

"She'll live, Mick," Jack said, watching me, "I was connected with them – she's in shock and a little bruised. That's all."

I started back towards the group.

"And the driver in the RV?"

"Extra crispy, I would imagine," Falkir mused.

I grabbed Jack by the front of his jacket and threw him against the broken brick wall; I knew it would come to this eventually. I grabbed him and thrust him up against the wall.

…Hold it, Mick…

Not listening.

"This was the whole problem that separated us in the first place! You can't use people like that, Jack! Kill them thoughtlessly?!"

He pushed me off of him.

"Well, *you* can't, Mick," he said, "But I'm not so worried about it, you know?"

I staggered back and pointed my sword in his face.

"Go for it, Mick," he sneered, "Toss a tactical advantage in a war you're already losing in the garbage. Just try it."

…He is right, Mick. If Jack or Falkir have information about Mannon, you need to hear them out, despite how much you despise them…

…Weak, Mick…Lichonus chided.

"Shut him up, Apostos," I said, aloud.

Jack raised his eyebrows and held up his hands.

"Okay, I get it…you're gears are slipping a bit. Maybe this wasn't such a good idea," he said.

…He is locked down again, Mick. It is getting harder to restrain him. He is feeding on your worst emotions to grow stronger…

It's only going to get harder. What are we going to do when we take in all the dark energy? Won't Lichonus get even stronger?

…Maybe, but I can draw on that power too so I can hold him back…

We'll finish this later. We're not out of the woods yet.

I sheathed my sword and exhaled.

"We can't stay here," I said, "That guy can track me wherever I go and I doubt we stopped him for long, based on how tough Apostos was."

"What would you suggest," murmured Falkir.

I couldn't believe he was here, within reach. I was sure that he had been the one who killed Simmi. After all the things he had done, how could I work with him without it coming to blood? We had such history…

"Portalling out won't do us any good," Jack said, "If he can track you. He'll just follow you into the next world. It might be easier to lose him in a cluttered place, like this city."

"Too many bystanders," I replied.

"Perhaps Father won't let the giant kill his people," Otomo said, "He is supposed to care about them."

"Well, as long as you can refrain from using them in suicide attacks, Jack, then maybe we can get away clean," I said.

"I'll try not to," he said, "But if it comes to the point where it's them or me, you know which one I'll choose."

"You're a real piece of work, Jack."

Falkir was looking back and forth at us quizzically, his ear cocked. The sound of police sirens started mixing with the car alarms.

"Excuse me," he said, "Who the hell is 'Father'?"

I shook my head.

"He's Apostos' boss," Jack said, "He created all the worlds."

I looked sharply at Jack.

"How the hell do *you* know that?"

"Penny," he said, "I didn't share all of what she told me with the rest of the Kingdom. Knowledge is power where I come from. Guess the dunce cap goes to you, doesn't it, Falkir, old chum?"

The sirens were getting closer.

"We need to go now," Otomo said, "Where are the others?"

"Safe," I said, "And until I decide what your new companions can do to help our cause, they'll stay that way. There's an entrance to a platform for a train that heads to another city in the north a few blocks away. We can head there for now."

Two police cars screamed from around the corner and pulled up to the warehouse ruins.

"Cops," Jack said, "I love cops."

He started walking towards the police cars.

"Wait," I said, moving to stop Jack.

He turned around, his eyes flaring green. Too late…

"Oh ye of little faith," he said, smiling at me.

The police cars slid up alongside us and the driver's side doors opened. The cops nodded at us and opened up the back doors. Their eyes were glowing. Jack climbed in, whistling.

"Coming?"

We piled into the two cars. I sat with Otomo as we rode to the rail platform.

"Care to explain your new travelling companions?" I asked.

"I don't know if it was luck, or fate, perhaps that has bound us all together, Mick. In truth, I was torn between my need to find and kill Jack and my word to you that I would return. I was travelling through Conway, a city I believe you know, when I ran into Flesh."

I remembered it. It was where I was run over and subsequently hospitalized. I didn't know the name until much later, when Casey and I traded stories about where we had travelled. Conway was a modern city and very crime ridden. Flesh's presence in the city did not surprise me…Casey said that Conway might have been on Flesh's home world, but we didn't know for sure.

"She was rounding up victims for Mannon's plans, using her wolves to terrorize and drive them into a portal she had created. I confronted her and she seized the opportunity to try and persuade me to help her free the others from Mannon…she was only doing his bidding out of fear, or so she said. We rescued everyone but Penny, so don't expect Jack to do much beyond save his own skin without some reassurances that we will rescue Penny from Mannon."

"True," said the cop driving the car.

Both of us started a bit. I forgot that Jack was actually here, hearing us through his puppets. Oh well, it would save a conservation later.

"Understood, Jack. What about Falkir?"

"He was to be sacrificed as well, or so it seemed."

"Maybe this is a trick. Flesh lured you in, got you to bring them back and into our midst so Mannon can kill us all in one go…"

"Flesh attacked Mannon at the last second, after Jack lost control of the sacrifices. She held him off while we escaped. It was honorable, Mick. Worthy."

"We can't afford to be stupid, anymore, Otomo."

"Is that why you won't tell me where the others are? You don't trust me?"

…Didn't this guy cut off your hand?...

Yes and he's travelling with the guy who stepped on the stump after and another guy who wanted to eat me the first time we met who also killed a good friend of mine What's your point?

…My point is that you need to be very careful in dealing with these people…

Careful? Well, there's a first time for everything.

"It's not that I don't trust you, Otomo, but I'm trying to keep my friends out of harm's way and I'm trying to figure out how to do that and still put the Kingdom's soldiers to good use against Mannon. Sorry, Jack, but that's just how it is."

The car started to slow down and the cop driving turned slightly towards me, his eyes glowing green under Jack's control.

"Is that it, up ahead?"

I looked out the window and saw a large, wide boulevard coming up with a staircase with gates on the front that led to a large trestle above. It was getting lighter now outside, towards dawn. If we didn't get on our way within the next hour, we'd be caught up in the morning commuter traffic and that would be disastrous if we were attacked again.

"Yes, that's it," I replied, "Make sure that these guys get far away after letting us off; I don't want to have to worry about their guns when they realize something's amiss."

"No problem…where's the nearest pier…" he muttered.

The cop winked at me and smiled. Jack was on his best behavior, for now. Somehow, I couldn't imagine Jack giving a damn about the cops otherwise.

We parked beside the station and Jack got rid of the cops while I summoned up some tokens to gain us entry. I stuck my sword in one of the trashcans, which got some funny looks from the others. I tossed the automatic in with it and nodded at the gates. A middle-aged woman dressed in black pants and a white shirt with the stenciled logo of the city rail system above the left breast stood in the opening beside a drop box. She seemed to not see, or not care about the fact that I just chucked a pair of lethal weapons in the trash.

…Mick, what the hell?…

Quiet, you. I know what I'm doing.

"Follow me," I said, giving each of them one of the tokens.

I dropped the token in the box and moved past the gates a few steps up the stairs. The others followed and we went up to the platform above. It was deserted, save for a few birds that flew back and forth between the supports for the large aluminum roof that covered the length of the open platform. Down the tunnel, I could see a light beginning to grow in the distance. I was suddenly hit by a wave of malice that surprised me with its intensity.

I looked around at my companions and my thoughts turned nasty. Falkir seemed to react to the change in me and backed away to drop into a crouch. I eyed him with a murderous glare. Jack reached into his jacket pocket and backed away as well.

…The sword, Mick, quickly!…

I know, I know.

I summoned the sword to me as quickly as I could. I felt its reassuring light flow back into my being and the incredible feeling of anger and hatred slowly ebbed away. That was close. I was getting worse…with Lichonus awake and stronger in power, I couldn't afford to be away from the sword; I would become more dangerous to my own people than Mannon. I put it back in its scabbard and sagged a bit as the reassuring strength of the sword flowed into me.

"What the hell is wrong with you?" Falkir growled.

I walked up to him.

"Well, after you and the Kingdom decided to mutilate me, I became host to darkness itself. Flesh's clumsy ministrations made it possible for the evil that Mannon perpetuates to get a foothold in me. Father gave me the sword to destroy the Kingdom and keep the darkness at bay. The remnant of the being I was before, a colleague of Apostos' called Lichonus, exists inside me now, along with Apostos himself after your former boss ruined his shell and drove him to move into me. Now, I'm host to powers that are conflicting, dangerous, and growing stronger with each passing moment. One says for me to save you, Falkir and the other says stick the sword in you and take your power to add to my own. That's what wrong with me, asshole."

The train rounded the curve in the tunnel and began to move alongside the platform. I looked at each of them in turn.

"What you have to ask yourselves, all of you," I said, "Is if you're going to get on this train with me, because there's no more time for infighting, as much as I'd like to indulge. The stakes are high and I'd imagine you think that there's no guarantee that we'll win, or even make a difference. I happen to believe that we can."

The train slowed down and a pair of doors slipped open close to the four of us. I stepped through and sat down at an empty table. Otomo joined me quickly. Jack shrugged his shoulders at Falkir and entered the train. Falkir looked down the empty platform for a moment. I knew how much he wanted to kill me and he knew where he stood with me. In the end, we both knew it would come to blood. It gave me pause as well.

"Better the devil I know," he said.

He got on board, taking a seat across from the others. Could I count that as a win? It was hard to know for sure.

We traded stories. It was the only way I could think of to get everyone up to speed, including Otomo's encounter with Flesh and my plans for Mannon. We took turns, each slightly reluctant to give away anything. I withheld where I sent the rest of the group…I didn't trust Falkir not to use it against me. I listened intently to his story, especially the bits about Apostos walking into the castle and Mannon's communication with the sinister power that spoke through Penny. The implications were ominous.

I knew that I couldn't trust Father after learning of how he betrayed us all to cover up his disastrous mistake. Now, I began to believe he offered up Apostos to Mannon as some kind of bribe to stay away. From what Falkir told us, Mannon wasn't interested in deals at all and whatever his end game was, it would be a bad thing for Father and his creations. The way it was going now, we had to force one side to lose without being destroyed in the aftermath…on one side, Father had planned on our destruction courtesy of the sword that I possessed, using myself as his agent and was now chasing us since we discovered how he had lied; on the other side, Mannon was hell-bent on revenge against Father using all means at his disposal, including any of his previous colleagues locked inside us as sources of dark power – we couldn't allow Mannon to win, or we would be obliterated. We had to force them to give us what we wanted, which was both peace and a home to make it worthwhile to keep.

The morning sky outside was brightening as the train rolled on towards the next city. More passengers had boarded and we were getting some strange looks. Most stepped around us…they seemed used to seeing the odd stranger amongst them, Still, Falkir's appearance and the sword strapped across my back were drawing the concerns of some officials, who were talking into radios and looking back and forth at each other and us. A quick flare of power from Jack dissuaded them from causing trouble and he marched them away from our car to give them time to forget why they were so concerned in the first place.

"Nicely done," I said.

Jack's eyes faded from green to his regular dark pupils.

"Not a big deal, Mick," he replied, "I figured you didn't want to get in a fight with these regular folk. Not that it would've been much of a fight…"

Falkir looked around at some of the passengers.

"Wherever we're going, there better be something to eat," he growled.

"Don't make me restrain you," Otomo said.

"Just try it, ghost-man," Falkir replied, "I have thought of an interesting way to make you disappear that has little to do with your power."

He patted his stomach with one leather-wrapped hand.

Jack sighed.

"Let's keep things civil," he said, "We've got bigger problems to tackle right now than petty grudges. Unless, of course, you have one against Mannon like I do, then the sky's the limit."

"I'd rather we not go off half-cocked and get devoured by Mannon, though," I interjected, "Working at cross-purposes to each other can only strengthen his plans, whatever they may be."

"What of our plan," Otomo asked, "What exactly are we going to do to stop him and make this crazy dream of yours a reality Mick?"

I leaned in close and Falkir slid in beside me. It creeped me out in a big way.

"Do tell," he whispered.

I held my hands out in front of myself, nearly a foot between them.

"This much space at all times, Falkir," I said, "Seriously."

He retreated a bit. I reached under the table and summoned up four little take-out boxes of barbeque chicken from the little place near the warehouse where Casey and I used to go and handed one to Falkir. I put the rest on the table.

"Will this keep you out of my face?" I asked him.

He ripped the box out of my hand.

"Silence," he said, "I'm eating."

Jack and Otomo grabbed a box and I joined them. The silence was welcome after nearly a solid hour of talk. Something missing…

I reached under the table and summoned a glass of dark ale from a bar that was beside the chicken place near the warehouse. Jack eyed the ale covetously as I brought it up from below and took a long drink from the glass. Sometimes, it was good to be me.

"Showoff," Jack muttered, gnawing on a drumstick.

The door to the car behind ours slid open and three teenagers with backpacks, two boys and a girl, came stumbling in and talking loudly. They kept on going along the corridor, heading up the next car. One of the boys, dressed in a long t-shirt, jeans and a red baseball cap covering a mass of golden curls, stopped to look out the window, his back to us.

"Enjoying the brew?" he said, loud enough so that everyone could hear him.

His friends kept on going, as if either he hadn't stopped, or they didn't know him.

"Lying down on the job and hanging with the wrong crowd can get a guy fired," he said.

I knew him. We we're in trouble.

The young man turned around and plucked a piece of chicken from Falkir's box. He bit into it, looking directly in Falkir's glowering eyes as he chewed. I had only seen the young man once and I felt Apostos flinch inside me. He was Sibelius, but probably not *just* Sibelius. He was Father's vessel while Father was on the worlds. He finished with the piece of chicken and dropped the bones back into Falkir's box. He dusted off his hands and became the image of the robed shepherd that I had met before, save for a very familiar gun belt that he dangled from one hand. He threw it on the table.

"There is nowhere that you can hide your friends that I cannot find them, Mick," he said.

"What have you done with them?"

He sat down across from us.

"They are safe right now," Sibelius said, "How long they remain that way depends on you and your fellow companions."

I felt Falkir tense. He was dangerous and would start a fight without any concern for bystanders. Ditto for Jack, promises notwithstanding.

"Get rid of the passengers," I said, "Get them out of here and we'll talk."

Sibelius nodded and everyone in the car disappeared, except for the five of us.

"Does that help engender your negotiating spirit?"

"Yes. I'll come with you if that's what it takes," I said.

"Everyone here is coming with us," Sibelius said.

Falkir snatched up a bone from his box, cracked it in half and put the sharp end of the bone against Sibelius' neck. Otomo phased through the seat and drew a small, retractable blade from his coveralls. Jack looked over at me and I raised my hand.

"I don't think they like the idea," I said, "And neither do I. You've always got to have things your way, Father. It's not going to happen."

Sibelius smiled, looking down at the bone splinter poking into his neck.

"You think you will have better luck this time, Falkir?" he asked.

"I've fought you before?"

"I left you broken last time…my patience with you is drawing to a definite close."

…Falkir did not know what he was fighting, Mick. He thought it was me when Father beat him down…

I didn't know that.

…That is how I died…Father took control of me after you sent me to spy on Mannon. He spoke with Mannon, they fought and he abandoned my body to be tortured…

…He's pretty rough on his creations, isn't he? Or maybe he sees us as mere toys in his little experiment…Lichonus muttered.

Quiet down. Something's not right here.

"That's too bad. I have no idea what you're talking about, little man, but I know for a certainty that you shouldn't have come alone!" Falkir said.

He put one sharp, clawed hand against to Sibelius' chest. He was beginning to dig in when he stopped, abruptly and sniffed the air. I started to smell something too…burning plastic and metal…it was getting warm in here!

"Oh, I didn't come alone," Sibelius said.

Near the front of the car, a large section of the ceiling collapsed in burning, melted chunks. Licks of silver fire still clung to the smoldering pieces. A robed figure in white leapt down from above, landing on one of the swiftly-cooling pieces of metal that used to be the ceiling. His head was shaven and he had a dark goatee. He had the familiar chainmail over his robes and shoulder pauldrons portraying roaring lions. When I saw his face, I realized I was looking at a dead man. Nicholas rose from the rubble, flexing his fingers as tiny flames danced on his fingertips.

The window behind our table exploded, sending Jack and I sprawling forward to avoid the debris. A strong pair of arms wrapped around me from behind and dragged me backward in a chokehold. I saw that the hands were feminine, delicate, and dexterous, but ended in golden fingernails sharpened into claws. I heard the slight tinkle of something as the attacker drew me close to her.

"How about you tell Falkir to let Father go, Mick," the voice said, "Or do we unleash the full force of our displeasure against you and the rest of the old gang?"

"So Father brought you both back," I said, "He must be getting desperate."

"Or maybe just trying to make amends for Mannon's acts against your little tribe," Sibelius said.

Falkir pushed Sibelius away.

"Lethia," he breathed.

She relaxed her hold on me.

"Julia," she said, "Hello Falkir."

"It will take a hell of a lot to make up for what you've done," I said.

"We are running out of time and it matters little what you believe about me. I have your friends and I will only release them when you have heard me out."

Father had remade Julia and Nicholas…could his hand have truly changed their natures, or were they merely the same monsters except now under his control? He had tipped the odds in his favour now and he had the rest of the group somewhere and would probably hold them until I cooperated with whatever he had in mind. I had to risk hearing him out, at least until I had a clear view about what was going on.

"Okay," I said, "But I'm not listening to another damned thing until you take us to where the others are being held. I need to know they're safe."

"Very well. Prepare yourselves."

Can you get us back from where he sends us, Apostos?

…If it is anywhere within the worlds, or in the palace, then I can use your ability to cross through to make a door to get back…

So as long as I have the power to cross, then you can bring us back?

…Yes…

Beautiful.

"I didn't agree to any of this!" Falkir howled, grabbing at my shirt.

"Don't be afraid, Falkir," Nicholas said, "It won't hurt a bit. Of course, I could be lying and it might be excruciating."

"You're all bastards! All of y—"

MICK

I've always wondered what Heaven would look like. I thought it would be like all the pictures from the ministries back home… the priests would come around every Sunday to harass my mother and father – there would be all these images of Heaven, clouds and bright, golden rays of sunlight and angels singing the praises of the creator with books of prayer in their hands. I imagined there would be a feeling of peace, maybe even a sense of belonging that would last forever. Little did I know that the creator of everything was a cheating, lying, control freak with little patience or sympathy for his creation.

I appeared in a giant chamber that had been described to me by Apostos when he told me of Father's betrayal of Mannon. I was on the floor of the palace in front of the dais on my knees. Beside me, Casey, Henri and Dakum lay…breathing, but not awake. There was a throne made of gold and crystal in the middle, through which green arcs of power surged and waned. At the top of the throne was a great lion's head with a crystalline globe in between its jaws…all the power seemed to flow to it. The globe shone brightly, illuminating a dais that flowed in steps down to the marble palace floor. The chamber had great arches for doorways to the towers that the shepherds used to watch over their assigned worlds, built from smooth white marble blocks that had never tarnished or cracked. The curves from the archways continued, overlapping, and crisscrossing each other until they formed a vaulted ceiling. In the middle of the ceiling, there was a twenty-foot dome made of some kind of crystalline material that absorbed the radiance from the throne – it glowed with power. Through it, I could see the shining stars of the real universe, beyond Father's experiment.

Upon the throne, Father sat. He was very different than when I met him before.

The good-natured wizened old man was gone. He was broad-shouldered, thick through the chest and evenly toned with muscle. He was clothed in simple white robes and a golden breastplate over chainmail. His skin was weathered as if he had stood on a mountain for a century, almost grey in tone. His hair was a long, flowing mane of white that rested on his shoulders. Father's eyes were a pair of emerald jewels, shining with the same ebb and flow that ran through the throne. They seemed linked, somehow.

Something was very wrong…I felt strange, as if something was missing…

…He's not here, Mick…whispered Lichonus.

What have you done?

…This is none of my doing…

"If you are wondering where your friend has gone, look no further than at my feet," Father said, softly and sonorously.

In front of him on the dais was Sibelius, standing over a prone form that stirred slightly, but did not rise. I recognized him immediately.

"What have you done?" I asked.

"Your savagery against Naxos has necessitated my retrieval of Apostos along with his restoration into physical form. If you will cast your gaze behind yourself, you will see the other consequence of your acts against me."

I glanced over my shoulder.

Along the curve of one doorway, manacled at both hands and feet and hung from hooks on the frame, were Jack, Falkir and Otomo. They were gagged as well and were glaring at me as if I was to blame. Flanking the doorway were Julia and Nicholas. They stood at attention, showing no concern for their former comrades. The only one I cared about was Otomo – why was he shackled with them?

"Why am I not locked up as well? I was the reason for him being there."

Father rose and stepped down from the throne.

"I need you, Mick," he said, "I do not need them."

I walked up to him. Sibelius moved up to join Father as I moved closer. They were very nervous up here, considering that Father was as close to being 'God' as anything was.

"What do you want?"

Father looked up at the crystal dome above us, out at the stars.

"I noticed you looking up at the stars out there, Mick," he said, "Look again and tell me what you see."

I looked up and then looked back at him.

"Is this some kind of a test? I—"

"Look again," he whispered.

I looked up again. The stars shone back at me through the dome that pulsed with green light from the throne. Each one was twinkling and…disappearing? It was unmistakable…like a slowly moving wave…swallowing up the stars as it moved in an arc across space. But some stars reappeared, as if something large was moving across them, blocking their light as it passed by. An eclipse?

"You see it, do you not?" Father asked.

It struck me with an uncontrollable sense of fear and powerlessness. This was the power behind Mannon, the Dark Sphere?

"I see it, yes," I said.

"Then you know of the Sphere and its power," a voice said.

I looked past Father and Sibelius to watch as a withered-looking man in white robes walked out from behind the throne carrying a staff that sparked and glowed with energy. His hair was iron gray and much of it was missing from the right side of his head. Deep scars marked the right side of his face and his eye was gnarled over with scar tissue. His one open eye was a droplet of quicksilver suspended in darkness and it fixed me with an unflinching gaze.

"But of course, I should expect no less from Mannon's favorite lapdog," he said.

…Pentalus…I thought he was dead…Lichonus muttered.

Apparently not.

"I only know what Lichonus has told me of it," I said, "My corruption was not voluntary, as his was."

…Ouch…

The truth hurts, asshole. I had a perfectly good hand before you decided to make a comeback.

"It is fitting then, that you make restitution for his crimes."

"Pentalus speaks true, Mick. He suffered greatly during the rebellion, as did we all. He serves me now as both chronicler and sage. Within him, much of my wisdom rests."

More players in the game; I was getting in over my head.

"It is time for you to fulfill *your* purpose," Father said, "I will be as direct with you as I can be. In the span of two hours, the abomination that you see above us will reach this palace and my control of the worlds will falter and will fall into its hands. Chaos, darkness, and the whim of the Sphere's apostle Mannon will rule all of my creation. I cannot stop it. It has established a foothold on one of the worlds and that is allowing the Sphere to draw closer. I have one last option to prevent the apocalypse from happening."

"Us," I said.

"You."

Pentalus raised his staff up in the air and moved it in slow circles. A pair of shimmering globes appeared and resolved to show two worlds. The globes grew in size until each took up a significant portion of the vaulted ceiling above us. The view began to zoom in to land-masses on each world, growing closer with each second.

"Watch," he said.

* * * * *

The ancient city, enormous and monolithic in construction, surrounded by dense jungle, was being pelted with hard rains and scoured by strong winds. Thunder rolled around above and flashes of lightning lit up the ruined avenues and alleyways. Dark forms moved among the rubble. Some were humanoid in shape and others more like beasts. They all howled with each peal of thunder and beat madly upon the stone walls. They were being driven by something that seemed to speak only to them.

In the middle of the city, under a crumbling ancient domed building supported by a ring of massive pillars, a woman knelt with her arms crossed against her chest in the center of the structure. Her face was tilted to the sky and she was mouthing words that were lost on the wind. Her hood had fallen back on her shoulders and her dark red hair was slick with the rain that fell on the city. As she spoke, the shadows in the chamber twisted and flowed like liquid and moved over her.

There were other forms there, each chained to one of the pillars. They were mere husks, drained of life and left to rot. They moved with the winds, lifting, and falling like driftwood in a rushing river. But something else moved with the wind as well…

It was like a stretched shadow that seemed to shorten and lengthen according to its own whim. A woman's face was visible once and then it distorted to become a demon's visage. Sketches of claws, wings and bones shifted throughout its length. It dropped and soared, moving around the perimeter of the ruins. It leapt up in a spiral above the structure and for a moment there was almost a solid form, a cloaked being crying out in torment, its clawed hands tearing at its body. Then it dropped again, breaking apart and becoming the shadow that lurked and thrashed among the dead.

* * * * *

Upon a great ocean that spanned the horizon, a single ship sailed south, its sails unfurled and rudder steady. Underneath it, something dark and enormous rushed along with it…a speed that belied a grace only bestowed by the oceans but could turn upon a whim into a force of destruction. The ship rode slightly higher, pulled along by the wake of such a power.

The sail billowed and swelled. On it, a black orb surrounded by twisting black tendrils wavered and shifted with the wind. On the decks, it was silent save for the sound of the groaning rigging…crimson stained the decks where men laid in the broken fashion in which they were slain, dusky-skinned men who had not seen death coming for them. A dozen bodies lay in succession from aft to fore.

Standing on the foredeck, his dark hair stirring slightly in the air, was a man swathed in darkness. His bare chest was writhing with dark tendrils that reached to caress his naked limbs, neck, and face. The black orb, twin to the one on the sail, seemed to pulse as if it was his beating heart. His eyes were open, but they were empty and black.

His grin was the only expression he wore, a row of pearly-white tombstones that curved to disappear into blackness at the edges. He gazed upward and opened his arms, closing his hands into fists. His mouth opened and he howled in a voice that was both his and another's, a human cry of defiance mixed with the hungry growl of something bestial and impatient sensing its prey.

MICK

"Well, that's terrifying," Henri said.

I looked down to see that my friends had been awakened during the horrifying glimpse Pentalus had given me of what was going on. Casey was rubbing at the side of her head with one palm and leaning on her other hand for support. I reached down and helped her up. Henri and Dakum looked stunned, so we helped them to their feet.

"Couldn't agree with you more, Henri," I said.

Casey gripped my arms.

"What the hell is going on?" she asked.

That was a damned good question. We all saw who was in the circle…Penny was at the centre of the darkness, the linchpin that held the ritual together that was allowing the Dark Sphere to draw closer to us. Mannon was using her to destroy us all. Worse still, she was being guarded by something that Mannon had formed from pure darkness, a wraith that would be tough to overcome. I doubted that even the four of us had the kind of firepower necessary to do it.

"I'm going to need help to do this," I said, "I need everyone…it's their fight too."

I pointed at the others chained on the wall.

"Let them loose."

"It would be unwise to do what you are asking…I know of your plan through Apostos' mind and I doubt it will work. Drawing the darkness from all assembled here might give you a fighting chance, but I have reservations about possibly creating another Mannon."

I let go of Casey and walked up the stairs a few steps to give it my best shot.

"You took one hell of a risk trying to use the darkness in your plans to quicken the pace of your experiment. I'm going to attempt to turn that massive blunder into something useful."

Pentalus frowned and looked at Sibelius, who also bore a look of concern.

They don't know. Not even now.

…Of course not. Father doesn't want them to know what he did…

"Mannon was like us once, our brother, as sickening as that is, but he has to be stopped," I said, "I need the same power he has to stop him."

"He is unknown to me," Pentalus whispered.

Apostos suddenly stood up, gasping. He looked around at us and settled on Father.

"Thank you, Father, for rescuing me from Mick's scheming."

Henri stepped forward to join me, bringing Casey up with him. He smirked at Apostos.

"Well, that's gratitude for you," he murmured.

"We'll make sure he doesn't stray," Casey said, "If he hesitates at any point while fighting Mannon, you can count on us to take him down."

I turned to Henri and Casey, trying to look shocked.

"Thanks a lot," I said.

"Between the four of us, I think we can manage it," Henri said.

"But not both Mannon and that circle," I interjected, "if you're leaving it up to us, Father, I suggest we send your ex-Kingdom people with the others as insurance. Both Jack and Falkir have good reason to stop that ritual."

Father waved his hand and everyone but he and I disappeared.

"Or we could try something else…"

Father grabbed me by the throat and picked me up off the floor.

"I have removed the audience for the time being. I know that you have learned of what happened between Mannon and I and I am aware of your talks with both Apostos and Lichonus. Did you really think he was yours to use as you see fit? Lichonus' arrogance has obviously been passed on to you. Do not try to raise your hand against me, or to cause dissension among the remaining shepherds loyal to me."

"Urk—"

"I do not require a reply, Mick, for anything other than utter acceptance will be a fatal error. If you or yours raise a hand against me, I will not treat them with the mercy that I did Mannon …I will burn you to ashes if you fail and I will take the gift that I gave each and every one of you and find more worthy vessels. I will take your consent as a given."

He let me go. I looked up from where I stood. Henri was frowning at me with concern and Casey was tapping her foot. Father stood where he was, a quiet smile on his face. It was as if we had never left the room.

"Yeah, we all hate Mannon," Casey said, "So let's go put a couple of holes in him."

"Okay, then. I'll need Apostos to drain the energy and put it in me," I said, nodding at Apostos.

He marched down the steps, his head held high.

"Oh, I will help you, Mick," he said, "But I am not your puppet anymore."

He leaned in close and whispered.

"I am no one's puppet."

I looked up at him. There was a strange look in his eyes, an almost human tension. He raised a hand and the chains fell from Falkir, Jack and Otomo. They moved over to join us. Julia and Nicholas followed at a distance. I saw Casey looking at Nicholas with a baleful glare and took her hand. I led her to the other side of the group.

"Are you ready to do this?" I asked her.

"What if you're wrong?"

I squeezed her hand a little and for a moment my confidence faltered. I wanted so much to live a normal life with Casey at my side…if something happened to her, this would all be for nothing. My home was with her, even if it was always while we were on the run.

"I'm not wrong, Casey," I said, "This is going to work, as long as your prepared to do what you have to do."

"I am," she said, "Just wish you'd come up with something less…suicidal?"

"Heh. I wish I did too."

Apostos moved up to me and took my arm.

"Do exactly as I say, traveler," he said.

"Of course, I—"

The palace shook underneath our feet and I saw a fissure open in one of the marble arches. The energy flowing through the throne dimmed and Father doubled over. Pentalus and Sibelius took a hold of him and led him back to the throne.

"Whatever you're going to do, do it now!" Pentalus hissed at us.

Apostos gathered the others in a circle around me, except for Falkir. There's always one.

"What is this? You know what's at stake."

He removed his kerchief and scarf, revealing his scarred face. He tossed them to the floor.

"When Flesh gave you your hand back, she used some of the darkness inside you. Now, it's part of you. What do you suppose will happen to me, a man who was restored with darkness, when you rip it out of me?"

"You never thought to bring this up before?" I said, exasperated.

"I didn't really believe you'd go through with it," he said, "And I know that you're not thinking about what will happen to people like me in the end."

Jack looked over at Falkir and grimaced.

"I'm out, too," he said, "I draw strength from what's in me and I'm going to need it all to get Penny back."

"Fine," I said, "I guess if you're not going after Mannon, then he's not going to suck you dry like a darkness-filled slurpy."

"Exactly," he said, stepping back to join Falkir.

The others took their places around me and Apostos, who stood beside me. The light was growing dimmer in the palace…I looked up to see that the stars were almost all eclipsed.

"Do it, Apostos."

Henri was the first. Apostos opened his hand in front of Henri's chest and slowly pulled it away. Henri gasped as thin tendrils of darkness slipped out from somewhere inside him and moved along Apostos' arm. He extended his other arm towards me and the darkness moved into me, the tendrils slipping like serpents.

The sensation was awful, the pain stifling as I absorbed Henri's darkness…something was there inside it…it was named Darius, the thing that had been Henri before and it fed upon his pain…I saw Henri when he was in his teens and his first lover…where was the pain in this? Then, the memory changed…an old woman held him down, a smile upon her face, a knife in her hand..'If you will not honour our family with children, then you will not sully us with your dalliances'…the knife dove down to below what I could see and I felt white-hot pain in my groin as she cut him…my god…I felt sick. How could a parent do that? How? I swallowed the pain and stayed on my feet. I looked up at Henri. He held up his hand for me not to speak.

"That's not for public consumption, Mick," he said, "It's old news anyway."

Apostos turned to Dakum and worked the same trick on him. This time, however, the darkness was like lightning and it leapt across Apostos in an arc to bury itself in my chest. Its name was Hespius and it fed on Dakum's pain…a boy nearly hobbled by the pain of his unusual growth in size, big for his age, was limping along in a dirt-poor village, using a piece of driftwood as a crutch…his leg was agony today…seven boys his age came out of an alleyway and began to chase behind him, kicking at his good foot or his crutch, trying to knock him down…he wouldn't fight, but kept on moving as best he could…they pushed him down to the dirt and spit in his hair, jeering at him and kicking at him as he struggled, never saying a word himself…one began punching at his face, his knees on Dakum's chest…Dakum swung his crutch and swatted the boy on top of him in the head…the boy fell from him, the others scattering as Dakum fought back…the tables turned and Dakum was on top of the boy…he brought the crutch down again and again and again on the boy's head…there was a crunching sound and a pool of blood spread from underneath his head…Dakum screamed and his eyes filled with tears…my heart ached with the guilt and pain that surged through him as he dropped the crutch and crawled away to weep. He killed the boy…What could I say? There was no right to it, no punishment worse than his broken heart. I looked into Dakum's eyes and felt a profound sympathy for his gentle nature. This universe seemed to rail against it.

"Keep going, Apostos," I said, "Let's get this over with."

Apostos nodded and turned to Otomo.

It was called Adrius and it was with Otomo all the time…it stood by him, on the shore of a tranquil sea at night, the waves gently lapping at his sandaled feet…a trickle of red crept into the water from behind him and another and another…the smell of smoke was in his hair…the debris behind him began with several men and women, each slaughtered and left in an undignified pose of agony…then came the wreckage, the broken furniture and accessories of a cultured people, all rendered into rubbish…then the houses, where flames roared into the sky and silence ruled over all…dead eyes looked into fires, eyes that resembled Otomo's in the merest detail…the wolves were gone, the strangers disappearing back to where they came…he raised his sword and positioned it over his stomach…a hand, smooth and out of place, not covered in soot or blood, stayed the sword as he moved it to end his life…a man, blond-haired and wearing strange clothes, whispered in his ear…'Not yet'.

How could he stand to be near them? Was an oath to me enough to hold him back from taking their heads? I had no idea how he held back from killing them. When I looked up at him again, he knew what I had seen and merely bowed slightly. I understood now, more directly, what he had said before about the way he lived.

"I guess you saved the best for last," Casey said.

She stepped over to me and kissed me.

"Whatever you see, just remember that I love you," she whispered.

She stepped back and Apostos put his hand on her chest. Casey gasped as her pain reached towards me through Apostos, a black mass of thorn-covered vines that wrapped around his arms and reached out to sink into my flesh…the thing called Bellerus, Casey's pain given name and form, screamed in my mind as I consumed it…the scene was familiar as she had described it…her father, dead at her feet, his murderers hung by their legs from a tree burst from the earth beneath the dusty tavern…Casey picked up her father's guns…her eyes were different than I'd seen them…calm…her irises were pin pricks…she reloaded the guns and went outside…this was different than she said…

A dozen men, women and children stood in the street, gawking at her as she came out of the tavern where the miracle had happened…there was a feeling to the air…heavy…Casey moved towards them and I recognized the feeling for what it was…doom. Casey blew the head off the first man and shot a woman in the back as she ran…Casey's expression didn't change…she shot them all, every single one in quick succession…merciless…the children she told to stay still, or she'd kill them too…

She finished with the adults and stood, breathing hard, in front of the children, who whimpered and cried, their little faces looking at her in shock…she was not much older than some of them…her words came out in a voice I'd never heard, even in the midst of battle…'Go…tell all of them what I done here. Tell them that if they get in my way, I'll leave their bodies in the dust'….she raised one of her pistols in the air and fired it…the children scattered…there was a groan behind her…the first woman she shot in the back wasn't dead…Casey walked up to her and shot her through the back of the head…

I didn't realize I was on my knees until I opened my eyes to see the others standing over me, their faces alight with concern. There was a terrible taste in my mouth and my body tingled with energy. I got to my feet and drew my sword. The others moved back. I gripped it as tight as I could. There was something moving inside me now, something terrible. I looked up at Casey…the horror on her face mirrored my own.

"Too much…"

…Murder, pain, darkness…

Shut up.

…Blood in the dust, cold eyes in the night…

Shut up, Lichonus.

…I remember why I fell…

I gripped my sword ever tighter, with both hands.

...Mannon gave me just a taste of what humans are, right at the core...so beautiful in their anger, so unrelenting in their wrath...you drown in blood, all the time...

"Mick! You need to go!" Apostos shouted.

My head cleared for a moment. Cracks were forming all through the palace and shards of marble crumbled to the floor. There was a trembling in everything. Julia, Nicholas, Jack and Falkir were gone. Sibelius and Pentalus tended to Father as he slumped on the throne. The energy was dark now, barely flickering. Apostos shook my shoulder.

"I will take care of things here, Mick," he said, "Go stop Mannon."

He walked up the stairs to join his fellow shepherds. A fine plume of dust swirled in the air above them. I rose from the floor and turned to my friends... their pain was my own now, their secrets...

"Prepare yourselves..." I said.

I opened a portal to Priddy. People were running in the streets and it smelled like smoke. We stepped through.

* * * * *

Apostos reached the throne and stood over Father. He smiled at Pentalus and Sibelius and leaned to take

Father's hands to comfort him. He took them tenderly and looked into Father's eyes.

"I remember everything," he said.

MICK

The streets of Priddy were swarming with villagers, fishermen and militiamen. People were calling out in alarm and a familiar bell rang in the square. It was usually only reserved for alerting the population to shipwrecks or storms. On the horizon, dark clouds crept towards the village. Women grabbed their children by the arm and ran into houses. The militia were helping people get into shelter. Where were my parents and my sisters?

"Mick…we need some weapons," Henri said, "These people have no idea what's coming."

"Right…" I replied.

I summoned up some energy, feeling the darkness swelling up inside. It was eager – it wanted to be used. My own energies were fighting to do what I was asking them to, pushing back against the darkness…I could feel Lichonus fighting me…

A trio of sabers…a black powder pistol…a pair of heavy gauntlets…this was exhausting! I dropped the gear to the ground.

"Here!"

Henri picked up one of the sabres and the pistol. Dakum slipped on the gauntlets…they stretched a bit over his huge hands. Otomo picked up the other sabre, testing it with a couple of swings.

"What about me?" Casey asked.

I turned to look at her. How could she have lied to me about what happened? What she had done was so out of character, so vengeful that I felt shaken to my very core.

…She is beautiful in a way that you can never understand…

You love the sound of your own voice, don't you?

"Take my gun," I said, holding it out to her.

She took the gun. I handed her the ammo. All the while, I could not meet her eyes. She grabbed my wrist.

"What's wrong?"

"Besides the end of the worlds?"

"Stop joking," she said.

"I'm not," I said, removing her hand from my wrist, "The universe doesn't stop and start with you and me!"

"Okay…" she said, backing up.

A single tear slid down her cheek. She turned away from me and wiped it. Why did I do that? I hurt her. I love her...

...Wrath, vengeance...you're adorable, Mick...

"Let's go kill this asshole," I growled, stomping off towards the harbour.

The others followed me. I heard Casey start loading the gun as she walked. Green sparks shot up from Henri as he began to alter the pistol with his power. Otomo wrapped the upper half of his overalls around his waist and walked bare-chested with the sabre in his hand. Oh shit. A young militia guard with a truncheon pointed at Otomo.

"It's one of the Hang!" he shouted.

I laid him out with a short, sharp jab to the nose. He dropped to the street.

"Needed that," I grumbled.

"What is a 'Hang'?" Otomo asked me.

Several members of the militia began following us as we walked.

"They're the enemies of Avalon, the big island that Priddy belongs to," I told him, "They look a lot like you."

"Mickey!"

The sound of his voice hit me hard…I hadn't heard it in years now, not since I left. My father, dressed in his navy cap, waders, and a black sweater, walked out from the doorway of a nearby house and took me in his arms.

"We thought ye were dead!" he said.

I gently pushed him back from me.

"Hello Da," I said.

He frowned and looked me up and down.

"Yer diff'rent now…" he said.

His gaze fell on the sword.

"Are ye some kin' a' sorcerer, son? Like in the old tales? The stories we heard…about the day you disappeared…"

"I am different, Da," I said, "But that doesn't matter now. Get the rest of the family and get them behind closed doors…it's no storm that's coming across the sea."

"Yer mother's gone, son," he said, "She left a year ago with the girls to Brighton."

"What? Why didn't you go?"

"I was waitin' fer ye," he said.

Oh my god…all this time…

"We don't have time for this, Mick," Henri said.

My father's eyes went wide when he saw what Henri was doing. Sparks danced across the weapon as Henri worked, tinkering with the pistol. Green energy began to glow from inside it.

"Are ye all sorcerers? What's all this Mickey?"

I sighed.

"Find somewhere safe, Da," I told him, "I'll find you later after it's all over."

"Okay, son," he said, "When you're ready, I'll be here."

He walked away, sparing a glance over his shoulder at us. He shook his head and kept on going.

"Mick…" Casey said, putting her hand on my shoulder.

"It's okay," I said, "We've got bigger problems…"

I turned back to the harbour. The dark clouds were much closer now. I could hear a mad howl on the wind…the darkness stirred inside me.

FALKIR

The winds whipped across the jungle where we entered the world, sending leaves and debris spiralling into the sky and throughout the trees. We were on the outskirts of the city, as close as we could get without landing in the midst of Mannon's minions. There was a low pulse, like a weak heart-beat thumping on the edges of my hearing. It came from somewhere to the east of us. Julia touched down to the ground in front of me, her white robes fluttering in the breeze. She drew a sword from within her robes. Nicholas stood on a pile of rubble a few metres away, his hands glowing with white-hot fire. Jack paced back and forth, his hands flexing and his knuckles cracking. His face was very tense. He had the smell of rage coming off of him, his testosterone pumping out of him like a furnace. I sniffed the air, drawing it in with my wolf's senses. I sat on my haunches on the fallen trunk of one of the huge trees that made up the jungle around us, my claws dug into the bark.

This was no mere assault that we were going on…this was revenge. If we stopped the ritual, then Mannon would lose. I only prayed that Mick failed to kill him before I got the chance to bury my claws in his belly…and then maybe do the same to Mick. No matter what little alliances we struck, it would only be temporary until I got my chance to pay him back for Flesh.

Flesh…

The memory of her was weakening me, turning me soft, when all I wanted to do was tear apart whatever it was that guarded Penny. But the image of Flesh fighting Mannon was stuck in my mind…it should have given me courage, but I felt empty instead. I hoped that my rage would get me through until all of this was done. Julia tossed the sword to Jack. It fell at his feet. He reached down and grabbed it, eyeing the blade.

"Let us depart," she said, "You three move across the ruins while I draw the attention of Mannon's creatures from above…I'll try to let you know if they're piling in to surround you."

"Follow me," I growled.

I bounded off the log and began to move towards the sound of the thumping beat. Jack moved in behind me, followed by Nick. We were together, if only to save our comrade from her monstrous fate. Being a monster, I understood completely how that could go terribly wrong.

"You know where you're going, dog?" Nick grumbled.

Hmm…nice to know things hadn't changed that much…I couldn't tear his throat out so easily now though.

"Yes…" I said, "Silence yourself before you get us all killed."

Jack hacked his way through the jungle as we entered the city. Nick was about to start burning his way when Jack stopped him.

"Save it for the enemy…they'll see the smoke," he said.

"As dumb as ever," I muttered.

Nick glowered at me as I bounded past him.

The ruins of the city were right in front of us. The beat was stronger now. Jack looked around and listened. Even Nick stopped as he heard the sound. I leapt onto the crumbled arch of a doorway leading into one of the avenues and waved for them to come forward. I scrambled over it as they came through.

I could see a large dark vortex that was spinning at the centre where we were heading. I could also see Julia, thirty feet away, much closer to the darkness. She had something large and dark in her grip and was tearing it apart with her bare hands. It was good to know she hadn't lost her touch. Little pieces of red and black fell from where she hovered as she shredded away. Several other shapes were jumping up onto the ruined walls near her to try and leap at her.

"This is *my* world," she screamed.

I chuckled as she plucked one of the dark things out of the air in mid leap and broke its back over her knee, her claws dug into its throat and groin.

Jack was the first to encounter the first of the dark things in our little group on the ground. It had come from around the corner to ambush us. It was barely recognizable as human…more like an ape dipped in tar. Its only weapons were teeth, claws, and madness. It succeeded in getting only as close as Jack allowed it to be. He hacked it down through the shoulder and the sword hit stone and rebounded as he bisected the creature. This wasn't the graceful swordsman I remember…Jack was careless over his concern for Penny. He saw me looking at him and glared at me.

"What?" he asked me.

I shrugged; there was no point in telling him something he already knew.

We made our way through the ruins, cutting, hacking, and clawing them down as we moved through. The thumping became louder as we approached where I presumed Penny and the circle to be. Julia was drawing a lot of them to her…for every one of them that we met, another didn't even see us as it moved to confront her, a few metres away from us in the air. I could feel the rhythm in my bones now, a dull thud that spoke of something huge, heavy, and powerful. I wondered if Mick and his group would have felt this at all…it seemed to be calling to me, asking me to turn around and go back, or surrender…fall to my knees before it. Not likely. I may be evil, but I'm not stupid. I would never be someone's lapdog again.

"What is that?" Jack whispered.

Julia screamed. Jack and Nick looked around at me and I bounded up and on to the nearest ruined piece of wall to see what was happening.

She was being pulled down by the weight of them…so many of the little buggers were trying to take her down into the midst of them, clawing at her robes, pulling at her hair, and holding on with a death grip when she eviscerated them with her claws. Julia needed help. Should I tell the others? It was an excellent distraction.

Small pangs of guilt twisted my stomach…I couldn't save her before when Mannon sucked the life out of her. That wasn't my purpose now, though; the Kingdom was dead. Flesh was dead and she was the only thing I had cared about save for my own hide…Mannon probably ate her up too, damn his rotten, empty hole. I dropped down from my perch.

"She needs help," I said, "More than a sword or claws can do."

Nick rolled his eyes.

"They're all over her, you fool! Get out there! We'll go on ahead to the ritual."

Nick took off without a word, his hands bathed with white-hot flame. I felt a wave of heat wash back at us as he began to burn the creatures. That left Jack and I…

We stepped out from behind the ruins and started walking down the alleyway towards the center of the city…we weren't too far away now…the huge pillar of darkness on top of the ritual was growing now. Jack pointed at the sky. It was growing brighter, nearly blinding as the gigantic form of the Dark Sphere drew closer.

Something broke off from the pillar and flew at us.

I pulled Jack to the ground as it swooped over us. I had an impression of dark claws, tattered robes like a winding cloth and a screaming mouth. It smelled like a charnel house, of death and decay. In its wake, tiny dark strips of cloth and bone flew along. But we weren't its target.

Nick never saw it coming.

We turned to warn him, but he was intent on burning the creatures off of Julia. It grabbed him and flew up into the air. Flames exploded around it as he fought back…in the shadow of the flames, there were claws and teeth working at him, tearing him apart as he fought against it. They moved close to us as they struggled…a face appeared in the midst of the shadows and the eyes swiveled to look directly at me.

No…

It swooped back up into the air.

"Get out of here, Jack," I said, "Finish what we came here for…get Penny."

He pointed at the struggle in the air.

"What about that thing?" he asked.

Thing? No, not a thing. I changed back into my human form but kept my claws nice and sharp.

"I've got this," I said, "Get her back, Jack."

Jack nodded and started off on a run towards the ritual at the center. I turned back to watch the darkness above me as it ate Nick alive.

* * * * *

Father looked up at Apostos with wide eyes and gasped as he pulled away. In his grip, there was a well-oiled revolver. He turned to Pentalus and blew out his accumulated wisdom out the back of his skull. The old man crumpled to the floor of the dais and his staff faded to a blackened piece of metal, inert and useless. Sibelius moved towards Apostos, but Apostos was quick enough to swing it back to point at Sibelius' face. Sibelius stopped dead and backed up.

"Why?" he cried.

Apostos pointed the gun at Father's head.

"Tell him, Father," he said, "Tell your new favorite son about all the things you did to the last one…tell him what you did to me!!"

"What are you talking about?" Sibelius asked.

"You left me to be tortured and murdered by Mannon after you were finished using me like you did him," he said, "You treat us like we are nothing to you – tools and test subjects that you can just throw away when you are done with them!"

"What do you want Apostos?" Father asked, "Revenge? You cannot hurt me with a gun…I have evolved beyond such frailty."

"Maybe you have and maybe you have not," Apostos replied, "the fact that Pentalus is not getting up again leads me to believe that you might be vulnerable…cut off from all the power you have reserved in the great experiment and weak from the influence of the approaching malignancy, you are merely what we see here…a weak, faltering old monster surrounded by his enemies and his victims."

"Will you risk it, Apostos? I think not. In your heart, you are weak—"

Apostos turned and shot Sibelius without a word. Sibelius put his hand to the wound, feeling the absence of part of his face. He toppled to the floor and his body tumbled down the stairs to come to rest at the bottom.

"This universe deserves a better god," Apostos shouted.

A loud report echoed in the palace and a blinding flash of golden light followed it. There followed silence.

MICK

The harbour was rocking and rolling with the waves as Mannon approached…the docks floated on the water and some of them were starting to tip from the magnitude of the waves rolling in as his ship approached. The villagers were scattering as the storm drew closer and the sky filled with a baleful brightness. The outline of the Dark Sphere was now visible in the sky…I hoped that the others were faring better than we were. I had my doubts that any of us would get out of here alive.

The darkness that I had absorbed from my friends was starting to thrash around madly inside me, looking for a way out. I intended to give it one soon…just not in the way that it wanted. I gripped my sword tightly, praying that it would be enough to hold off the darkness until it was time.

Henri wandered over to me as we stood on the docks, readying ourselves.

"I wonder how the others are doing," Henri shouted at me, above the wind, "Doesn't our success here have a lot to do with how successful they are?"

"If they break the ritual, then probably Mannon will lose a lot of his power…this is all part of his attempt to hit Father while he's vulnerable.

Meanwhile, I guess we've got to hit him as hard as we can and keep him busy."

"What the hell is that thing in the water?" Casey asked.

"No idea," I said, "But you can bet that it's going to be nasty…the seas are teeming with unpleasant crap since the melt."

"Well, since you've got the only weapon that can probably hurt Mannon personally, then maybe the rest of us should deal with the whatever-it-is?"

"I need Casey beside me," I said.

Henri rolled his eyes.

"Just get a room…" Henri said.

"Not like that!" I said.

Casey folded her arms across her chest.

"Are you sure?"

"I mean…yes, like that," I tried, flustered, "but also…we are in the middle of a fight here!"

Casey's hat flew off and was lost on the wind as the gusts hit us. The storm was really close now and I could see the ship nearly a kilometer away from the shore. The darkness was getting angry, now.

…This is going to be such fun, Mick…

You've really got to shut up now, Lichonus. I'm not in the mood for your jabbering.

…Mannon's already won, Mick…you just don't know how yet…

Again, be quiet.

My mind raced…putting Mannon to the sword was firmly in my mind…whatever happened after was purely a bonus.

Henri pulled out the pistol I had given him and pointed it at the incoming ship. He squinted down the improvised sight that he had created for it, a sequence of brass rings that grew smaller as they approached the end of the barrel. He adjusted a couple of the new little knobs and switches and the pistol seemed to hum and whine…green light shone out of the end of the barrel.

"Henri…what did you do to the crude, but reliable technology I gave you?"

He grinned, fiddling with one of the knobs, giving it some kind of fine adjustment.

"Just tell me when he gets within about ten metres or so," he said.

Casey took a couple of steps back.

"Oh, come on," Henri said, "I'll admit that it's hastily made, but it's hastily made *by me.*"

Casey stayed where she was.

Henri frowned and grumbled.

"Totally unappreciated…"

I looked back to see if the others were ready. Dakum was flexing his hands and pacing in impatience, his eyes glancing between the horizon and where Henri was standing.

"Maybe you should move back a bit," I whispered to Henri.

"He's pissed, isn't he?" he replied.

"Yeah."

Henri sighed and moved back a metre or so. I turned to see Dakum nodding at me. He was so protective of Henri. I nodded back.

Otomo was getting downright scary by comparison…he was kneeling down on the docks, his entire body was flickering, pieces of him turning ghostly, others becoming real, then ghostly again. The sabre I had given him was laid out before him. His eyes were distant and were glowing with energy. He didn't seem to see any of us…I remember seeing the same look on his face when we found Apostos in Trelain. What was going on in his head?

…He's getting ready to die, as you should…

Nothing's decided yet.

…Believe what you want...

The ship was close now…I could see Mannon standing on the bow. Mannon was surrounded by dark tendrils that lifted and writhed around his body. His eyes were fixed on me as he drew closer.

"Fire, Henri," I said.

I felt the heat lance out of the front of the pistol from where Henri stood beside me. It was brighter than anything I'd ever seen, a focused beam of energy that raced towards the approaching ship. Henri pulled the pistol down and the beam sliced through the sail, the railings and down through the hull and below. I dreadful cry of pain and anger rocked us from below the ship. Mannon jumped out of the way of the beam and landed on a dock a few metres away.

The water heaved underneath the ship, sending the vessel keel over stern into the sea. The great, monstrous shape of a kraken, a giant squid with many long tentacles rose up from below, the creature's skin covered with dark ichor. Its body was the shape of an anchor and say high on the water, supported by the tentacles as they flayed about. There was a deep burn scar, high on its body, where the beam had sliced and cauterized it. It was raising its tentacles in the air to fight us…each of the tentacles had cruel hooks and suckers oozing with ichor. This thing was made to kill us.

"Don't let it touch you!" I cried.

Mannon moved quickly, crossing the docks on his own legs, and being lifted along by the tendrils. Henri leapt back to join Dakum and Otomo. Casey moved around from behind me and put a couple of rounds in Mannon as he moved towards us. He laughed as the bullets hit him and didn't slow down at all. He was having way too much fun with us. He reached me as I hoisted my sword up to hack him down.

Mannon's tendrils lashed out, forming long spikes that threatened to impale me. I dodged underneath them and cut one of them off. The touch of the sword was electric, burning the tendril like acid as the severed piece dropped to the dock and began to sizzle. Mannon stepped back. Casey came around beside me and pointed the gun at Mannon…you had to give her credit…she wasn't giving up.

Meanwhile, Henri, Dakum and Otomo were under attack from the kraken. Henri was using the beam to slice at it, which was angering it further. Dakum was trying to keep the tentacles from slicing Henri apart, slapping at them with the force of his hands. Otomo had risen from the docks, sword in hand and was walking slowly and steadily towards the kraken…what the hell is he doing?

"Not doing so well, are they?" Mannon said to me.

"Well enough," I said, "It's the end of the worlds, after all."

"This would be a good time to give up, Mick. If you and your people lay down your weapons and walk away, I will promise you amnesty on any world which you choose to inhabit."

Why was he so damn confident?

"Shitty deal…you know what happens if we stay anywhere for too long."

"That's your problem."

The tendrils reformed, gathering up his arms into a large sword made of pure darkness.

"Last chance," he said.

"Go to hell, Mannon," I said, moving to engage him.

Our blades met and each meeting brought sizzling shards from his sword flying in all directions. The darkness kept on filling them in as we clashed, forming over the damage as quick as I could hack away at it.

"Otomo!" came Henri's cry from behind me.

I looked over for a brief moment as Otomo became ghostly and dove directly into the great body of the Kraken.

"He's not going to like it in there," Mannon said.

It was just enough of a distraction.

Henri's beam sliced through Mannon's right arm, severing it clean. Mannon screamed as the member exploded in a splatter of darkness.

"Gotcha," Henri said, blowing smoke off the end of his pistol.

FALKIR

The thing that was once the woman I cared for most in the world tore apart our old comrade in quick succession. The flames in the darkness stopped flaring and there were no white robes showing as she devoured the rest of his being. I would feel bad for Nick for dying twice trying to fight Mannon, but I was left with the fallout of his failure. I knew I wasn't walking away from this. I stood still, waiting for her to come to me.

The darkness sailed down through the air, the shards of bone clattering in the breeze like a wind chime as she floated down. I looked over to where Nick had been burning the creatures trying to save Julia. There were burnt corpses everywhere...some stirred, some twitched. On top of it, streaked in red and black gore, was an arm lying limp, the lily-white flesh of it in deep contrast. The nails on the end of the hand were golden claws. It was very still. I didn't know if Julia was dead, but she was out of the fight.

The darkness swirled in front of me and collapsed upon itself until a form began to take shape. Her form was slender, but shapely still. It was draped in a cloak that ended in tiny bones. Her hands were great, chitinous black claws that hung at her sides. From underneath the shredded remains of her hood, her face was visible…it was only half there, one eye remained in darkness. The other beheld me, unblinking.

She turned her head and leaned in towards me. One claw reached out and touched my ruined cheek. It was cold. The claw traced down my form, ending at my own claws. I reached out, slowly and put my hand on her cheek, or where her cheek seemed to be. It was cold and hard as stone; it felt like a mask.

"I'm sorry I couldn't save you," I said, hoping that there was enough left inside of her to understand.

She frowned and seized my arms with her claws.

"Flesh…release me…help me kill the bastard."

She shook her head slowly and I felt her claws tighten around me. Was there nothing left of her?

She embraced me and I felt the warmth leave my body. I winced as her claws dug into my back, piercing my flesh, and digging in…it was painful and sensual. There was something left of her, but there was something new inside …something I knew very well. It was hunger…mad, predatory hunger.

"Don't let me live without you," I whispered.

The face that was not a face disappeared and became a skull.

I wouldn't dream of it... it seemed to say.

I felt all that I was draining away as she fed on me…this wasn't cruel, or painful…it was the end…peace…

* * * * *

Jack ran towards the dark pillar at the centre of the city. Several creatures jumped out to take his life, but they were all dispatched in savage desperation. He almost tripped over the corpses as they fell in several portions. As he entered the ring of pillars that encompassed the ritual area, the corpses twisting on the wind rose from their drifting slumber and came towards him, hissing and moaning. The blade ripped through them as they reached with skeletal claws at Jack. They fell easily, but there were many. Jack bowled through them, abandoning thoughts of protection and entered the inner circle.

Penny knelt, her hands at her sides, her head now sunken to her chest, her hood fallen over it. She was still speaking, but drowsily now…Jack heard her as she whispered…*'the sea will break, the Apostle will rise…the devourer will eat her young…the king, withered, will pass into memory as the sun rises…*Above her, a nimbus of darkness danced around her head.

Jack scrambled to his feet, kicking at the corpses that clawed at him in their attempts to drag him away. He looked at Penny and tackled her. There was a great roaring and the stone pillars shook as the darkness exploded from the dark pillar and began to hurtle back into the sky. The corpses collapsed into dust. The winds began to die down as Jack cradled Penny in his arms.

She stared up at the sky, her eyes focused on the outline of the Dark Sphere as it began to retreat. Her eyes were as dark as the night sky. Her gaze shifted to Jack and she smiled at him.

"Are you okay?" he asked her.

"I feel fine, my love," she said and rose to her feet.

She stretched and looked down at herself. In one deft movement, she shrugged off her old clothes, which were torn and filthy.

"Um…" Jack said, smiling at her naked form.

She smiled as well and ran her hands down her body. As she did so, darkness like silk swirled out of her palms and wrapped around her body. They became a silk robe with a hood that she eased over her dark red ringlets. She sighed as the garment settled over her. Turning around to Jack, she reached down and extended her hand.

"Come, my love," she said, "We have a lot of work to do."

He took her hand and they disappeared from the world.

MICK

Mannon staggered back from us, gripping his oozing stump. While he did so, the great form of the kraken heaved and twitched in the water, sending waves that threatened to bowl us all over. Mannon floated up and away from us. Casey steadied me as the waves tried to wash us both away. Dakum dragged Henri back with his power. Otomo was still inside the thing and it looked like he was giving it one hell of a stomach ache. Its thrashing became more violent and we struggled to get back to where Dakum and Henri were.

The kraken's misshapen skull exploded in a shower of blood and black ichor and the ghostly form of Otomo emerged, covered in foulness that had worked its way through his body…I could see tiny tendrils in his ghostly form…inside him. He had somewhere lost the sword and his arms were soaked with gore up to the elbows. He had literally hacked and yanked the thing apart from the inside. He collapsed onto the docks and became solid again. The dead kraken sank beneath the waves, leaving a slick of ichor behind. Otomo stared back at me from where he lay. He began to shudder.

"Otomo?"

"A debt paid in full, a vow fulfilled," he whispered.

Otomo became still. The darkness had devoured him as he had crippled Mannon's monster. He cried out and green energy flared from his eyes, then faded. He was gone. I wanted to go over to him, but Mannon was moving again. He laughed and ichor collected from the wound and solidified to form another arm from the stump.

"I'll add his death to all the things you've done to hurt my people," I said to him.

"Such a long list," he mused, "Let's add to it."

Mannon soared at me on tendrils of darkness. Casey and I ran forward and we met him in the middle of the docks between us, my sword raised to strike him down. He halted in front of me and shook his finger at me, scolding. I moved to bring the sword down on his skull.

It stopped. I stood there, frozen in my move to strike him, unable to bring my arms down. I tried again, but the sword stopped before it got close to striking him.

…I think not, Mick…

Are you insane?

…No, just loyal…

Mannon flicked at the sword with one blackened finger.

"Having difficulties, Mick?" he asked, "Thank you, Lichonus."

He waved his hand and a solid wall of darkness formed behind Casey and me, cutting us off from Dakum and Henri. I saw flashes of light and heat from Henri's pistol immediately hit the wall, but nothing happened. We were trapped inside with Mannon.

"Lichonus would never strike me, Mick," he said, "We served together, as you well know. Father's days are numbered and I'm not going to let some freakish, nasty little human with a taste of power interfere with my plans for my—"

He trailed off and looked up at the sky where the outline of the Dark Sphere was sitting. It began to retreat.

"No!" he cried, "You can't do this to me! Not again!"

"Those crazy Kingdom bastards," I said.

Mannon looked back at me. He grimaced and his hands became a pair of blackened sickles.

"It doesn't matter," he snarled, "You're going to die anyway!"

"For once, I agree with you completely."

I brought the sword whistling downward and reversed it, burying the blade in my chest. The emerald on the pommel flared with energy and I dropped to my knees.

"Mick!!" Casey cried.

…AAAAAAARRGGHH…

Goodbye, you bastard.

Lichonus screamed and rolled inside me, thrashing to get out as the energy obliterated him from my soul. My blackened hand melted away, leaving the stump. The pain was impossibly huge and I collapsed onto my side. Casey grabbed me and put her hand to the wound, trying to stop the blood. I was already getting cold…

"No, Mick, come on…" she moaned, "This was a bad idea…come on…"

In every relationship, there is an element of risk. For Casey, I would risk all. I felt some of her energy flow into me and I gasped as the pain kept me awake. I watched, helpless, as Mannon moved closer, his sickles cutting at the air. His grin was triumphant and hideous.

"Oh, don't worry little girl," he said, "You'll join him soon enough."

Tears flowed from Casey's eyes as she raised her pistol. She screamed at him and unloaded her entire clip, blowing chunks off his shoulders, face, and chest. He laughed at her and slapped the gun out of her hands with one of his sickles. His wounds began to close into solid flesh from the darkness inside of him. His hands reformed.

"My triumph, my vengeance may have been temporarily delayed," he said, "But I am still kicking."

He grabbed Casey. I tried to move my arms to pull her back, but they only twitched instead. Mannon pulled her close like a lover and his mouth opened wide to reveal teeth dripping with black ichor.

"And I am very, very hungry."

He moved to bite her and gasped. He looked down to see that Casey had put her fingers deep into the open wounds on his chest. He grinned at her as darkness oozed from his wounds on to her flesh.

"Kinky, but if your gun can't hurt me, why do you think your fingers can?" he asked her.

"I don't want to hurt you, Mannon," Casey said, "I want to heal you."

Mannon eyes widened.

Casey's eyes flared brilliantly. Power surged down her arms and entered Mannon, climbing over the ichor in waves. Mannon's entire body lit up as the darkness seemed to be drawn out of him and into her arms, only to be changed into the green light…his veins became to glow with energy. The black sun on his chest writhed and the black tendrils seemed to be trying to escape from their confinement on his body. They burned with the energy she was pumping into him as she fed on his death to create life. The blackness all over him receded and his eyes burst with energy. She threw him off of her and he fell to his knees. The black wall behind us collapsed.

Casey swung around and grabbed the sword in my chest. She pulled it free and I felt the cold enter me once again as my blood spilled on to the docks. She brought it around in an arc and put it against his neck.

"This is *not* over," he said.

"For you, it is," she replied.

Mannon smiled. Casey swung the blade and his head toppled from his shoulders. His body collapsed to the ground and began to wither and turn to dust. Casey tossed the sword on top of his corpse and knelt down beside me. Henri and Dakum joined her. All my friends…

Casey put her hand on my chest again and I felt the wound close. Warmth flooded back into me and I reached out to take her hand with my remaining one. She smiled. Then she slapped me across the face with her other hand.

"Your plans really suck sometimes, you know that? Next time, you get to watch me get stabbed and see how it feels!"

"Oh shit," Henri said, running his hands through his hair, "I hope there's not a next time."

Dakum just stared at us.

"What?" Casey asked him.

"You people are crazy," he said.

MICK

We stood over our friend. I had mixed feelings about him…Otomo had been a pain the ass for me and sometimes a pain in other parts, but he had also been loyal unto his death. Maybe that was the real difference between the people that I had come to call my friends and family and the Kingdom…both tribes were bound by similar fates, but it was how we chose to face our fates that made us who we were. Otomo chose loyalty to us over his vengeance for those who destroyed his people. I hoped that, wherever he had passed on to, it was somewhere that was worthy of his sacrifice.

Henri was the first to walk away. Dakum followed him. I took Casey's hand and led her away.

"What happens now?" she asked.

That was a good question…

"Yeah," Henri said, "I was kind of wondering when the parade and the booze were going to show up…shouldn't Father be kissing our asses right about now?"

"There's one way to find out," I said.

I started speaking the words that opened the portal between worlds. The portal opened and I could see the marble floor of the palace and the dais beyond it…something was lying there at the bottom. As I stepped through with the others, I faltered and nearly tripped. I recognized what it was that lay on the floor, or rather, who. Sibelius looked up at me from the marble stones, his eyes open and half of his head missing from a gunshot wound. Apostos spoke from on high.

"Welcome back, everyone," he said, "There's been a small change in plans."

MICK

Apostos sat on Father's throne. The throne pulsed again with power and a ring of green energy coruscated back and forth across Apostos' body from the globe in the lion's mouth. To one side of the throne, I could see Pentalus' body sprawled on his back with a familiar wound to the head, his mouth open in a frozen look of shock. One of Casey's revolvers lay at the foot of the throne. There was no sign of Father at all.

"What have you done, Apostos?"

"What I had to," he said, "What I felt was right."

"Where's Father?"

Apostos shook his head.

"You killed him?" Casey asked.

"With your gun, no less," Apostos replied, "Handy little weapon, really."

"You killed a god with a gun," Henri said, "Huh."

"He was separated from the bulk of his power," he said, "You should all be thanking me; he never would have fulfilled his end of the bargain…it was not in his nature to make deals with lesser beings."

"And you took his place," I said.

"Unfortunately for me, yes. As you can see from the way the energy is flowing around me, something is very wrong."

An arc of energy from the globe flared brightly and struck the dais, reducing a big chunk of marble to ash. Henri made an alarmed sound and ducked behind Dakum.

"I know when an experiment has gone awry," Henri said, "That was the throne venting energy, wasn't it?"

"Very astute, Henri," Apostos said, "You see, I was not meant to contain the amount of power that the experiment around us represents. Right now, all I am is a little man with his finger in the dam as it threatens to blow."

"How the hell do we fix this?" I asked.

"As luck, or maybe fate, would have it, Father created a whole bunch of really interesting beings in the form of what he once was. Of course, none of them evolved to become powerful enough to inherit his power, but he did tamper with a number of them, altering their essences to hurry the process along a bit. Hence, your little tribe. One of you has to switch places with me and soon."

What a day…

"Okay," I said, spinning around to my friends, "Who wants to be God?"

"This is insane!" Casey said, "What happens if one of us doesn't do it?"

"Without proper control, the energy will lash out and obliterate all the worlds and everything will end for us," Apostos said.

He cried out in agony and a bolt of green lightning shot out of his body and blew up an archway.

"Sometime soon would be good," he gasped.

The flow of energy in the throne began to pulse faster. Crap…I grabbed Casey's hand and kissed her cheek.

"You have any problem with being married to a god?" I asked her.

"Mick, no! You have no idea what this will mean! You don't have to do this!"

"I disagree," Apostos said, "heartily."

"Wish me luck," I said, walking up the steps to the throne.

Casey tried to stop me, but I kept on going. I couldn't let my friends down…this burden would be mine…Otomo had chosen to end his life in service of our cause…how could I do any less…risk anything less than all I was? Apostos stood from the throne and put his hands on either side of my face.

"Be good to the worlds, Mick," Apostos said, "They need a god that gives a damn."

Apostos seemed to erupt with energy and it all flowed down his arms into his hands. He started to come apart and he cried out as he flattened his palms against my face.

The energy from all the worlds flowed into me. There's….so…much….I—

MICK

On a hill there is a tree. In the tree there is a leaf. On that leaf there is an insect. In the insect there are one and a half million cells. In each cell, there are a billion atoms. In each atom, I am there. I am the atom, the insect, the leaf, the tree, the hill, the continent, the world. I am every world. I am the wind that blows across it or doesn't. I am the waters that flow over its surface, or I am the dust that lingers when the waters have receded. I am the hand that puts the spin on each world so that there is day and night. I am the inheritor of everything.

I am a man.

I forget my keys. I make bad calls. I get sick. I choose where I go and what I do. I choose who I spend the time with that has been given to me. I share myself and I take in what others share with me. I am all of us…even the worst of what we are, for that is as important as the best that we do. I am a man who knows love.

I am a god.

I am Mick and I am a god who was a man. Before that, I was a shepherd. I am a shepherd now.

No more marble palaces…no more worship.

I am the formless space. I am the dirt that fills it. I am the grass that grows on that dirt and the water that falls upon it. I am the stone and wood that forms houses for my tribe and for my wife. I am the blue sky and the sun that shines down on those houses. I am the mountains in the distance, the rivers that rush down through them and the tall trees that lay at the foot of the mountains. I am a promise, fulfilled.

I am Home.

TO BE CONTINUED IN…THE DARKEST HOUR!

Manufactured by Amazon.ca
Bolton, ON